THE LION TAME

Peter Dickinson was born in Africa, within earshot of the Victoria Falls. When he was seven, his family moved to England, where he later graduated from Cambridge. For seventeen years he worked on the staff of the magazine *Punch* before starting his career as a writer – which he knew he was meant for since he was five years old. His first book was published in 1968, and since then he has written more than fifty novels for adults and young readers.

Among his award-winning children's books are *City of Gold* (Carnegie Medal), *Tulku* (Carnegie Medal and Whitbread Children's Book of the Year), *AK* (Whitbread Children's Book of the Year) and *The Blue Hawk* (Guardian Children's Fiction Award). He lives in Hampshire.

Books by Peter Dickinson

THE
LION TAMER'S
DAUGHTER

Peter Dickinson

MACMILLAN CHILDREN'S BOOKS

First published in the United States of America by Bantam Doubleday Dell
in *The Lion Tamer's Daughter and Other Stories*

First published in the UK 1999 by Macmillan Children's Books

This edition published 1999 by Macmillan Children's Books
a division of Macmillan Publishers Limited
25 Eccleston Place, London SW1W 9NF
Basingstoke and Oxford

Associated companies throughout the world

ISBN 0 330 37164 9

1 3 5 7 9 8 6 4 2

A CIP catalogue record for this book
is available from the British Library.

Typeset by SX Composing DTP, Rayleigh, Essex
Printed and bound in the UK by Mackays of Chatham plc, Kent

Before all this happened I'd have told you there wasn't anything special about Melly, apart from her being a bit dopey sometimes, and maybe the business with the yellow dog, but that was a once-off.

I don't know that we'd have picked each other for friends if our mums hadn't been friends too. They'd got to know each other waiting for us outside junior school, and found we lived only a couple of streets apart, so they'd fixed for just one of them to collect both of us, turn and turn about. Then Melly's mum, Janice, got the chance of a full-time job and my mum, who just worked mornings, said she'd have Melly till Janice got home. That way we saw a lot of each other and got used to each other being around, a bit as if we'd been brother and sister, I suppose. We were both only children, and Melly's parents had split up.

We went on together from Ashley Junior to Ashley High. Sometimes we were in the same classes, sometimes not. We each had our own lot of friends and we didn't hang about together at school, but we'd help each other out over anything we needed and Melly came home for tea with me most days, long after it would have been all right for her to have her own key and go back to her own house.

My mum and dad were crazy about sailing, and ever since I could remember, Friday nights, they'd load me and the cats and themselves into the van and drive half the night to a little cottage we had at Penmaenan, in Wales, where they kept their boat. (We weren't rich people, mind you. The cottage was pretty primitive, and the boat was all they ever spent money on.) Sundays it was back in the van and all the way home to Coventry. Holidays were always sailing too, as much time off as they could get from their work.

It took them a while to get it that I wasn't that keen on sailing, even on fine days, and I loathed it when it was cold and wet. So some weekends they'd ask Melly along and she and I'd muck around at the cottage and Mrs Pugh next door would keep an eye on us while they went out in the boat. Other times I'd stay back in Coventry at Melly's place. So all in all you could say I knew her pretty well. But if you'd asked me to give you a list of my friends, I'd have started off telling you the three or four other boys I mostly hung around with, and then maybe I'd have said, 'And Melly, of course.' Or maybe I'd have forgotten. Same with her, I should think.

We didn't have rows, that I remember. We were just easy with each other, and that's about it.

When I say Melly was sometimes a bit dopey I don't mean she was stupid or silly. Most of the time she was ordinary, bright but not brilliant, better than plain but not pretty, with black hair and a bit of a foreign look, Italian or something. She was a chatterbox, and hung out with a gang of girls who were that way too, and when they got going it was like a flock of geese squawking away. You'd hear them coming round from the gym, fifty or sixty it sounded like, cackling and shrieking, but when they got to the corner you'd see it was just five or six of them, all talking at once and rolling their eyes and shrugging and waving their arms around. Body language, it's called.

But every now and then Melly would go dreamy and faraway, and you'd pretty well have to pinch her to bring her back, and she'd still be sort of dazed as if she'd only just got out of bed, and grumpy too, which wasn't like her. It happened enough for one of the teachers to get the idea she might be on drugs. We had a bit of that at Ashley High, but we knew who they were, and my lot didn't have much to do with them. Nor Melly either. She was too careful for that sort of thing.

The stuff with the yellow dog happened a bit before what I've just been talking about – our last year at Junior, it must have been. One of Melly's crowd, Karen, had just had a birthday and she'd been given a puppy and her mum had brought it along so she could walk it home. Melly and I and one or two others tagged along. Mum wasn't picking us up that day and we were supposed to go straight home, but Karen's wasn't far out of our way and the puppy was a beagle and dead cute.

We got to the edge of a big open place, playing fields and such, when this other dog came lolloping across. It was a large, bony thing, yellowy-brown. It didn't seem to have an owner. It probably just wanted a sniff, the way dogs do, but Karen's mum got all anxious and started trying to shoo it off.

It didn't like that. It stopped in its tracks and looked at her. It put its head down and the fur on its shoulders stood straight up and it began stalking slowly towards us, growling in its throat as it came. All of a sudden it looked really scary.

Karen's mum started to back off, gabbling to Karen to pick the puppy up and telling the rest of us to get behind her. Then Melly walked past her and faced the dog.

'Beat it,' she said. 'Go on. Beat it.'

The dog stopped and looked at her. It was still growling and the hair was still up on its shoulders, but you could see it was making up its stupid mind.

'Beat it,' said Melly again, not yelling or anything, just talking like a tough teacher who knows you're going to do what he tells you, so you might as well. She was still walking slowly towards the dog.

It looked away, still growling, and then it swung round and lolloped off.

Karen's mum didn't say thank you. In fact she began rabbiting on at Melly about being stupid, and dogs like that are dangerous, but Melly smiled at her and said, 'It's all right. My dad's a lion tamer.'

That shut her up for a moment, so we two said, 'See you' to Karen and the others and went off our way, but we could hear Karen's mum telling them about dangerous dogs for quite a distance.

'Is he really?' I asked her. 'Why've you never told me?'

'Yes, but Mum doesn't like me talking about him,' she said. 'If any of the others ask you, tell them I said that just to stop her going on at me.'

A bit before I was fourteen, Dad died. He was sitting in his chair, talking about this rugby match we'd been watching on TV, when he stopped with his mouth wide open. For a moment he just stuck there, but before we could do anything his arms jerked up – you could see he couldn't help it, it was as if they were being yanked around from outside him – and then he was jerked to his feet with his face gone all sort of sideways and his tongue sticking out, and then he gave a couple of shudders and keeled over half across the chair. Mum was screaming. I got to the phone and rang for the ambulance.

The men did all the things you see on TV, but I knew it wasn't any use. He was dead already. There hadn't been any warning. He'd never had a heart attack before, not even a twinge. It just happened like that. Bang, you're dead.

Mum didn't know what to do. That's not just a way of talking, it's what I mean. I'd never caught on before how much Dad mattered to her. He was what she was for. Take him away, and she wasn't for anything. (Except me, I suppose, but I'm not sure it wasn't because I was *his* son, mainly.) Sailing, for instance. I said they were both crazy about it, but the fact is she was crazy about it because he was. If he'd been crazy about gardening or something, she'd have been crazy about that too. It wasn't that he was selfish and made her go sailing – she really loved it because he'd shown her how to love it, and neither of them could understand why that didn't work with me.

Anyway, she wasn't going sailing without him, so she sold the boat and the cottage. And they'd lived in our house in Coventry ever since they were married, and she didn't want to be reminded of him every time she opened the door, so she sold that too. I've forgotten to say that her job was helping with the costumes for the Royal Shakespeare over at Stratford. Theatre people all know each other and I think she must be pretty good because she got herself a new job almost at once, working for the Scottish Opera in Glasgow. So we left Coventry and went to live up there.

One other thing before I go on. My dad was a good careful guy who liked to do things right. He was pushing forty when he married Mum, and she was only nineteen, so he'd taken out proper insurance for her. Not that he'd expected to die that young – he was only fifty-five – but it meant that she had a bit of money to help us get by.

Glasgow wasn't that bad, in fact I found the change easier than Mum did. She'd got her work, but she didn't seem to want to go out or make friends or anything. Some of the kids at school tried to give me a hard time about being English, but not that I couldn't handle, and I soon found a crowd to hang around with. Our new house was nice, not in the rough bits you hear about but out on the edge, a place called Bearsden, with little farms and steep hills and a golf course close behind. I hit it off with a boy called Ken who lived fairly near. He was nuts on birdwatching and summer was coming on, so we did a lot of that.

But it was amazing how much I missed Melly. There wasn't anything special about her I missed; it was not having someone like that around, someone just there. I'd get home from school, evenings, and put the kettle on and without thinking I'd get two mugs out of the cupboard . . . The one Melly used had an elephant on it. I put it right at the back of the shelf, but I still found myself looking for it.

This is going to sound silly, because we weren't in love or anything, Melly and me, let alone being married seventeen years, but missing her like that gave me a bit of an idea how my mum must be feeling. We wrote to each other a bit, and we tried telephoning, but it wasn't the same. We didn't want to chat, we just wanted to have each other there. I'm guessing about Melly. She didn't say and neither did I. It's not the sort of thing you *can* say.

Scottish Opera doesn't stay in Glasgow all the

7

time. They go on tours all around Britain, and abroad sometimes. The costumes are all made before then, but they have to take a couple of people from the wardrobe department along to do last-minute fixings. Mum doesn't usually do that, but that first year, just as they were starting off to do a fortnight in Edinburgh at the beginning of the tour, one of the people got hit by a van and had her leg broken, and the other one got stranded on holiday somewhere, so Mum agreed to do the Edinburgh fortnight. I stayed over at Ken's and stopped in at home every evening to feed the cats and check the post and the phone messages.

At the weekend Ken did the cats for me while I went up to Edinburgh by coach to be with Mum. She'd said to pick her up at the theatre, but when I found her they'd got a crisis on, with a stand-in soprano who was a good bit shorter and fatter than the one the costumes were for. I said OK, I'd leave my bag with her and go out and bum around Edinburgh for a bit and be back lunchtime. Someone said to go and look at the castle, which seemed a good idea, but I took a wrong turn and found myself moseying up Princes Street. If you don't know Edinburgh I'd better describe it. There's this sort of canyon running into the middle of the city. It's laid out as a park, with the castle along the top on one side and this famous street on the other, so that you can walk along looking out over the park at the battlements and stuff up on the skyline. There's steps and paths going down and up the

other side. There's a lot of stuff for tourists –
buskers with bagpipes, tartan souvenirs, that sort of
thing – and classy shops the other side. It's worth
seeing.

I walked along as far as the last lot of steps and
started down them. They zigzagged to and fro.
Turning one of the corners about halfway down, I
saw a couple of girls coming up. One of them was
Melly. She was chattering away like she used to,
with all the body language going. I stopped dead in
my tracks and stared. Then I saw her hair was all
wrong and she was wearing a mass of make-up and
smoking a fag, so I stared some more. I couldn't
help it. She was staring back by now, but she'd have
done that anyway, the way I was gawping at her.
She said something to the other girl, who stayed
where she was while the one I'd thought was Melly
came stamping up the steps – she was wearing Doc
Martens – straight at me. I was still thinking how to
say sorry when she said in a low, furious voice,
'Hey! You were in that effing boat when I was
chucking up!'

She didn't say 'effing' of course. Most of the kids
I know swear a bit, some of them every third word,
like breathing. Melly was one of the ones who'd
sorted out it was cooler not to. Anyway, I knew
exactly what this girl was talking about. It was one
of the weekends Melly had come to Penmaenan and
it had been pretty good sailing weather and Dad
had talked her into giving it a go and she'd been as
seasick as hell.

'That's right,' I said. 'That was at Penmaenan.'

'That was in an effing dream!' she said, still furious.

'It was real, Melly,' I said.

'Melanie,' she snapped. She did a double take and stopped being furious.

'How come you ken my name?' she said.

Yes, *ken*. But she had a funny accent. Edinburgh people talk different from other Scots, but this was something else.

'You're Melly – I mean Melanie – Perrault,' I said.

'Perrault,' she said, putting me right. It's a French name, because Melly's dad was French. This girl made it *sound* French.

'What's your name?' she said.

'Keith,' I told her.

'What more do you ken?' she said.

(Really she said something like, 'What mair dae ye ken?' but I'm not going to try and write like that. I hate reading dialect, and I wouldn't get it right, and anyway that would make her sound much too Scots. She had this other accent – French, I guessed, from the way she'd said her name. What I'll do is use some of her words, like 'ken' for 'know' and 'aye' for 'yes'. She sometimes said 'wilna' and 'dinna' instead of 'won't' and 'don't' and so on, but mostly she said them the English way, except when she was excited or upset. I'm not going to try and do anything about her accent – it was too weird. What's more, it shifted about. Sometimes it was much stronger than others, but it was always there a bit. While I'm at it, I'll leave out most of the swearing, but she didn't do that all the time either.)

So what else did I know? I didn't know where to begin.

'Your name's Melanie Perrault, and you live, you used to live, in Coventry, like I did, and you went to Ashley Junior with me and then Ashley High, and we'd walk home to my place after school because your mum . . .'

She grabbed my wrist so hard that her nails dug in. She'd been frowning and shaking her head about what I'd been telling her, but now she stared as if she was trying to look right into my head.

'Promise this isn't a put-on,' she said.

'Promise,' I said.

She thought. 'All right. When I'm at . . . your place, I get to have my own mug.'

'That's right,' I said. 'The one with the elephant on it.'

'And yours is a green one with white spots,' she said.

'It got broke in the move,' I said.

'What's my ma's name, then?'

'Janice.'

'Janice,' she said, trying it out. I guessed she'd known about the elephant but not about Janice. She was pale now under the make-up, and trembling. She took a long suck at her fag and threw it away.

'Wait there,' she said, and went running down to the other girl. They talked for a bit. The body

11

language was different. The other girl was obviously fascinated and wanted to join in, but Melanie wasn't having any. In the end the other girl came on up the steps, pretty sulky, staring at me as she went past. Melanie came up behind her, a bit calmer now.

'Probably thinks I've gone on the game,' she said.

'Funny kind of place to start,' I said.

She looked at me for the first time as if I was human, and smiled. The way she did it was so like my Melly when I'd said something to amuse her, my heart almost stopped.

'Got any money?' she said.

'A few quid.'

'Buy me a Coke?'

'OK.'

She took me to a place up another lot of steps, in a sort of shopping mall, with booths and big windows looking out at the castle. Soon as we were sitting down she lit up again. The pack was empty so she threw it away.

'It's got to be there's two of us,' she said. 'Twins. When they split up they took one each and they never told us about the other one. What's she like, then?'

'Spitting image of you,' I said. 'Except she doesn't smoke and she doesn't do make-up, much.'

'Right little pious snob, then? Bet she doesn't dress this way, neither.'

I haven't said that as well as the Doc Martens she was wearing fishnet stockings with tears in them and a fake leather mini and a shiny red jacket and she'd got her hair cut short and spiky.

'She would, too, if Janice let her,' I said. 'Tell you what, a bit before we came north she was having one of her dopey fits and she was drawing in a dreamy kind of way and when she'd finished she showed me. "That's me looking at myself in the mirror," she said. It could've been you, now. Lipstick and all. The fag, even.'

'Jesus!' she said. 'Just after Christmas, this would be?'

'Around then. We came north January.'

'I bought this lot with my Christmas money, and I remember what a kick it was trying it on in the shop, and feeling effing great looking at myself in the mirror until this cow of a woman came and told me it was no smoking in there. She tell you about that?'

'No. But . . . she made a sort of sour face and tore the drawing up.'

'Yeah . . . You said dopey fits.'

'When she sort of goes away for a bit.'

'Me too. That's when I get these dreams. Not like night-dreams – they're something else – but . . . Jesus! She'll have been watching what I've been up to! Not just watching, neither – doing it along of me. Like me being sick in that effing boat!'

She looked a bit shaken by the thought, but then she laughed – Melly all over again.

'Well, she'll have learnt a thing or two,' she said, 'and maybe she wouldn't have learnt them in . . . Coventry? Right? I knew it had to be England, some place. OK, then – tell me about my ma. Skinny, with red hair, right?'

'No, that's my mum. Janice has got dark hair and she's not so tall. She's not really fat, but she's a bit that way. She's sort of neat, though. Nice clothes, but a bit boring, suits and things – but that's for her job. I don't remember I've ever seen her in trousers.'

'That's my ma! I thought she was some kind of aunt. Go on, everything you can remember.'

'You didn't even know her name, then?'

'Papa gets mad if I ask. Real mad . . . You know . . .'

I could guess. Well, I settled down and started telling her everything I could remember about Janice, which was quite a bit. Thinking about it, I wasn't surprised, if Melanie'd only seen them in these sort of dreams, that she might have thought my mum was really her mum. Mum's a feeling person. If someone's in trouble, she's right there with them in their trouble. Janice is more of a thinking person. If someone's in trouble she'll look things up in books and ring round and find what's the best way to get them out of their trouble, and then she'll put it on to her PC and print it all out for them with numbers at the start of each bit. They'd have made a great troubleshooting team, together.

I took a while telling her. Then she borrowed some money off me and went to buy herself more fags. Yeah, she was two years under age, if she was Melly's twin, but she knew her way round. While she was gone I checked the time and it was getting on half-past twelve, when I'd told Mum I'd be back at the theatre, so I was up at the bar paying the bill when Melanie came haring back and shoved what I'd lent her into my hand.

'I've got to go,' she said. 'I'm in dead trouble already. How do I get to talk to you again?'

'I'm coming with you,' I said. 'What's up?'

'I work in the restaurant Saturdays, and I'm on at twelve. He'll beat the eff out of me. Got enough for a cab? Pay you back – honest.'

She was panting it out as we raced up the steps, and there was a taxi just finished being paid off. I jumped out and stopped him driving away. (It made me feel good, valiant-knight-to-the-rescue stuff. Silly, sure, but it happens.) She gave the address to the driver as we got in.

'We've got to sort out about meeting up,' I said. 'What's this about the restaurant? Can't I just come there . . .'

'Chrissake, no. I told you about Papa.'

'The one who's going to take it out on you for being late?'

'Right. Mind you, he wilna let anyone else lay a finger on me.'

'But Melly says her dad's a lion tamer.'

'He used to be, but something happened at the circus – I dinna ken what, he wouldn't say – and he chucked it up. Sold his lions and came to Edinburgh and got a job at Annie's doing the bar. He married her after a bit. I waitress when I'm not in school . . . Do something for me?'

'Sure.'

And I meant it. No messing around whether it would get me in trouble or clean me out. I'd have done what she wanted as if she'd been Melly.

'You'll have to act up a bit,' she said, and leaned forward and asked the driver to stop. She got out and scuffed around in the gutter for a handful of dirt and rubbed it into the side of her face, using the wing mirror to see what she was doing. Then she dirtied her forearm and knee and took off her jacket and scuffed it along in the gutter and put it on and got back in. While she was doing this I found a scrap of paper and copied down our hotel number, which Mum had given me, and our number and address in Bearsden. She glanced at them and tucked them into the pocket of her jacket.

'Ta,' she said. 'Right. I've been knocked down by a bike and you've been looking after me. You're new in Edinburgh? OK, there's this steep little street, cobbles, in behind the station. Doesn't have a pavement. You're coming up and I'm coming down – it's a way I could've been taking back to Annie's – and there's this van just come up past you and a bike coming down, and the stupid sod on the bike thinks he can get between me and the van, and he can't. Got it? So you've picked me up and got a cab and brought me home because you're a good guy, right? Don't overdo that, mind. You better pay the cab off in case Papa comes rushing out to grill him about where he picked us up, but then you look like you were hoping to get your money back. Do that for me, Keith?'

'I'll give it a go, sure.'

It wasn't that far. We stopped in another touristy kind of street, only this one was all gift shops and Scottish woollens in genuine little old houses. Melanie stayed in the cab while I paid the driver.

I helped her out of the cab and she put her arm round my shoulder and I put mine round her waist and she hobbled along beside me into an alley and there was the restaurant, Annie's Genuine French Bistro, next to a haggis bar. It didn't look too bad. I'd hardly got the door open when a square, tough-looking woman looked up and came striding towards us, but before she reached us a man came rushing out from behind the bar, shouting at Melanie in French. They both stopped when they saw the state Melanie had got herself in, and I started explaining to the woman about the accident I was supposed to have seen, while Melanie mumbled away to the man in French. The woman calmed down at once, but the man stayed very het up, but not in your standard comic-Frenchman way. He was short and skinny, but his head didn't look like a small man's head. I don't mean it was too big for his body, but it had this heavy, hungry look, with high cheekbones and deep-set eyes. I could see he was still furious, but in a frustrated kind of way, because the people he wanted to take it out on, the cyclist and the van driver, weren't there for him to get at.

'I don't think she's really hurt,' I told the woman, because I knew Melanie wouldn't have any bruises to show. 'She's just pretty shaken up. She wasn't making any sense at all at first, and then it took us a while to get to where we'd find a taxi . . .'

'Waiting to be paid, is he?'

'He's gone. I've paid him. It was three pounds fifty with the tip. I hope that's all right.'

'Course it is,' she said and went off to the till.

I looked to see how Melanie was making out. The man had grabbed a chair and sat her down, but as soon as he saw me turn he drew himself up with his head held back like a soldier on parade.

'I give you most profound gratitude,' he said.

He had a very strong foreign accent, but he spoke slowly and solemnly, so that I could pick up what he was saying.

'That's all right,' I said, and took the chance to tell him, too, about Melanie not being hurt, just pretty shook up.

He nodded.

'You will accept luncheon?' he said. 'On the house, naturally.'

'I can't, I'm afraid,' I said. 'I'm supposed to be meeting my mother. I'm late already.'

'Very good. In that event you will bring your mother to dinner this evening. I would wish to express my thanks to her also. Excuse me.'

A customer was getting impatient at the bar. He strode off. The woman who'd gone for the cab fare was dealing with two new customers, so I'd a few seconds to talk to Melanie alone. I wanted to see her again, but I didn't want any dealings with her dad, if he was the sort to beat her up, and certainly not to take free meals off him. But when I told her she grinned Melly's quick, wicked grin.

'That's worked out terrific,' she said. 'You've got to bring your mum round so I can see her. The food's pretty good, tell her.'

'I don't think she can. There's two shows Saturday, and she'll be on for both of them. What are you doing tomorrow morning?'

'Mass, first off, and then nothing. But I've got to be back here twelve.'

'Mass' shook me. Melly didn't go to church at all, and nor did we.

'Meet you for another Coke, then?' I said. 'Same place, ten?'

'Great,' she said. 'If you get to bring your ma along here, tell her to keep her mouth shut, whatever.'

She'd glanced past me, then muttered this last bit. Now the woman came back with the cab fare and I explained about having to go now, and how Melanie's dad had asked me to bring Mum that evening, but I wasn't sure if she could because of her job, and would she tell him. She was really nice about it and got me a card and told me to ring if we were coming and made me feel she really wanted us to. Then she took Melanie off to somewhere behind the bar and I went back to the theatre.

I was over an hour late, but Mum isn't good at time and she hadn't missed me. In fact I found the opera crisis was still full-on and she was kneeling with her mouth full of pins by this woman, fitting her dress, while the woman was belting out practice notes in a voice you could have heard up at the castle, and not paying any attention to Mum at all. It was only half an hour to curtain-up and there was still another costume to go, so I went off and bought myself a sandwich and brooded about what had happened, and got nowhere except that it was weird but it was terrific having Melly around.

OK, that sounds stupid. She wasn't Melly, she was Melanie, and it wasn't just smoking and swearing and going to Mass and talking French and stuff. She was someone else. Her whole life was different. There was no way she'd fit in with my life the way Melly had, any more than I'd fit in with hers. She'd have been bored stiff and I'd probably have been scared stiff. But it wasn't any good telling myself that. Melly was who she was – a new, exciting sort of Melly.

Second time I got back to the theatre the opera had begun and Mum and another woman were stitching away like fury getting the costumes sewn for the other two acts.

'I'm really sorry about this, darling,' Mum said. 'Especially when you've come all this way to see me. But it'll be done in a couple of hours and Alicia here is going to be a saint and take over for the evening, so you and I can go out and do something together.'

'That's great,' I said. 'I've got us a free meal.'

'That's nice, darling,' she said, and then – oh – a good ten seconds later, 'What do you mean, a free meal?'

'I met someone who works in a restaurant and got her out of a jam,' I said. 'It's all right, Mum – nothing crook about it. And she says the food's good. It's supposed to be French.'

The woman at the restaurant sounded pleased when I called her, and I got the idea they were going to lay things on a bit for us, so when Mum said, 'Is it the sort of place we dress up for?' I thought maybe yes. I hadn't brought much, but I got myself tidy, and Mum can be a very pretty woman when she bothers, which she did. It must have been about the first time since my dad died, and it was nice to be taking her out looking like that.

It wasn't too far from the hotel, so we walked. When we were just about getting there I said, 'Now, listen, Mum. You're going to recognize someone. And you're going to work out who someone else is. It's going to be a bit of a shock, but you've got to act normal.'

She stopped and faced me.

'Will you please tell me what this is about?' she said.

I hadn't told her anything, not even the story about the bike and the van, because that would have meant lying, and I wanted her to see Melanie for herself first. Besides, I was having fun. I grinned.

'It's all right,' I said. 'Promise. You'll see.'

'Oh, God, you remind me of Mike sometimes,' she said. (Mike was my dad, of course.)

I was glad we'd dressed up, because they really rolled out the red carpet for us. The woman was

21

watching out for us and stopped what she was doing and came straight over. I'd guessed she must be Annie so I introduced her to Mum, and then Melanie's dad showed up and did his soldier trick and gave her a stiff little bow and said, 'I am Gustave Perrault, Madame.'

She knew what to do at once. She gave him her hand to kiss and said she was enchanted to meet him and she was Patricia Robinson.

'Madame, I felicitate you upon your son,' he said. 'He is an English gentleman.'

I could have sunk through the floor, but Mum smiled and said, 'I'm glad you think so,' as if she meant it.

Annie's wasn't much more than a tourist caff, really, but they showed us to what was obviously their best table, in the window. They'd laid it out with candles and ranks of cutlery and extra glasses, and Melanie's dad – Monsieur Perrault I'm going to start calling him – went to the bar and came back with a bottle of champagne which he poured into three glasses and then looked at me and offered me some in mine. I looked at Mum and she said, 'Well, since it's a special occasion,' and he gave me half a glass.

The four of us were just starting to drink each other's health when Melanie showed up with a plate of little pastry things to nibble. Mum had her glass to her lips, pretty well brim-full, but she didn't spill a drop.

Melanie shook Mum's hand and smiled her

Melly smile and said, 'Keith was really good to me this morning, Mrs Robinson.' She was so terrifically on her best behaviour I wanted to giggle. Monsieur Perrault poured about a thimbleful of champagne for her and we drank their health and then Monsieur Perrault said, 'We have, with regret, the restaurant to conduct this evening, but Melanie will arrange that you have all you require.'

Mum smiled and thanked them and they pushed off. As soon as their backs were turned Melanie let out a long sigh of relief and we both had to bite our lips to stop the giggles.

'Will somebody please tell me what's going on?' said Mum. 'It really is the most amazing likeness. And your name's Melanie Perrault? You must be our Melly Perrault's first cousin.'

'For God's sake be careful,' I whispered. 'We think they're twins, but she's not allowed to ask anything about her mother. Hold it. He's turning this way.'

Mum didn't blink. She smiled across the room and raised her glass to Monsieur Perrault.

'We better tell her what's supposed to have happened,' said Melanie.

'Only it didn't really,' I said, and we explained about the van and the bike and so on, making it seem as real as we could, and Mum reacted as if she was believing every word. In the middle of this Monsieur Perrault came and said that they had chosen a meal for us, but we could have something else if we wanted, so of course we said we'd be happy with whatever they gave us. He seemed very struck with Mum, which made him even more stiff and gallant and difficult not to laugh at. Mum was wonderful with him, playing along with him and getting it just right, not overdoing it. In fact I thought she was rather enjoying that, but I also got the idea something was bothering her.

'Keith's alone in Edinburgh,' she told him. 'He hasn't got anyone his own age to talk to. Will it be all right if Melanie sits with us when she isn't busy? I'm afraid Saturday's a bad time for that.'

'But of course,' he said. 'Already these arrangements are made. She has just the two other tables she must attend.'

He poured her more champagne with a great flourish and went back to the bar. Melanie had to go too, to serve someone else. Mum waited for her to get out of earshot.

'Tell me something, Keith,' she said. (She never calls me Keith unless it's serious.) 'I gather this story about Melanie being knocked down by a bicycle isn't true.'

'I'm afraid not,' I said.

'But you told me all this was above board. It seems to me we're getting a free meal – and they've gone to a lot of trouble over it – on false pretences. I hope we aren't. I wouldn't like that at all.'

This absolutely hadn't struck me, I'd been so swept along by the adventure. I couldn't think what to say.

'It wasn't like that, Mum. Honestly. Wait till I've

. . . And anyway, he'd have beaten her up for being late. I mean beaten.'

I hadn't said it on purpose, but it's one of the things she really minds about. Anyway, it did the trick.

'I'm sorry to hear it,' she said. 'I was finding him rather attractive.'

'Mum!'

'Champagne is wonderful stuff, darling,' she said, with a look that didn't let me guess whether she was teasing or not. Either way it would have been the first time since Dad died.

'Listen, Mum,' I said. 'You're not to go cold on him. You've got to find things out. If he comes back, talk to him in French. Ask him how he got to Edinburgh, that sort of thing. Get as close as you can to when Melanie was born without letting him see that's what you're interested in. I'm not just being inquisitive. It's important. Listen. This is what really happened . . .'

I started to tell her about that morning, from me going down the steps and seeing what I thought was Melly coming up. Melanie came back and joined in two or three times, but she kept having to dash off and wait, so it was mostly me. I didn't finish till Melanie was clearing our main course away. Mum didn't say anything, so I asked her what she thought.

'I believe every word you've told me, darling,' she said. 'And I don't understand it at all. But let's wait till Melanie comes back.'

It didn't work out like that. First, Melanie was

too busy to talk, and then, when we'd finished our sweet, Monsieur Perrault came and asked Mum if she'd like brandy or liqueur. I've forgotten to say he'd given us red wine with the meal, which Mum said was pretty good, though I didn't like it much. When he came back he'd got a large glass of brandy for himself, and asked if he could join us. Mum said, '*Enchantée, monsieur,*' and he was delighted and answered in French and she batted it back to him and they got going. She speaks pretty good French. She actually met my dad while she was au-pairing out there, so she didn't have any trouble keeping her end up. I speak a bit – better than most kids my age – but going that fast they lost me, so when Melanie came back we talked about the obvious things, mostly music. I knew she'd like Hole and P. J. Harvey, because Melly did. We didn't get any chance to talk without Monsieur Perrault hearing, but when we were saying goodbye I looked at her and she gave a little nod to tell me the arrangement to meet next morning was still on.

We walked home. As soon as we were round the corner I said, 'You see, they've got to be twins, haven't they?'

'I don't want to talk about it now,' said Mum, 'not after all that wine. I suppose you're seeing her tomorrow?'

'Ten o'clock,' I said.

'Do you mind if I come too?' she said. 'I'm sorry – I expect you want her for yourself, darling, but I've got things to tell her which I'd rather say directly to her. I can't stay long. I ought to be at the theatre by half-past ten. Is that all right?'

'Yes, of course,' I said, though it wasn't.

The place where we'd had the Coke didn't open till twelve on Sundays, but Melanie was waiting on the terrace, leaning on the railing and looking at the view. She was wearing a black skirt and a white lacy blouse and a black cardigan and no make-up. Oh, yes, and little shoes like dancing slippers. Apart from her hair she was a real Miss Prim. She didn't look at all disappointed to see I'd got Mum with me.

'Hello, Mrs Robinson,' she said. 'I'm like this because it wasn't worth going home after Mass.'

'Melly calls me Trish,' said Mum. 'I can't stay long, but I've got something to tell you. Is there anywhere we can sit?'

We were lucky and found a bench in the sun.

'Is it OK if I smoke?' said Melanie.

Mum made a face. She smokes a couple of fags a day, but doesn't like to see kids doing it.

'I don't have to,' said Melanie and stopped getting her pack out.

Mum touched her arm. 'I'm sorry,' she said. 'Please smoke if you want to. This may be hard going for you.'

'Thanks,' said Melanie, but she didn't in fact light up.

'Last night I said to Keith that I believed every word of what you'd both of you told me,' said

27

Mum. 'So the first thing to say is that there's no way you and Melly can be twins, Melanie. I'll tell you why in a moment. I thought you might be cousins. Suppose your father had a brother, possibly a twin brother, they might both be lion tamers – circuses are very family affairs, I believe. Then these extra-ordinary . . . visions you and Melly seem to have of each other – I'm assuming she has them too, because she does have these absent fits – they might make a sort of sense. But last night I got your father to tell me a bit about himself and he was quite open about it. The main thing is that until four years ago he lived and worked in a travelling circus based at Arles, in the south of France . . .'

'That's right,' said Melanie.

'Melly was born in a circus based in Arles,' said Mum. 'Her birthday is the nineteenth of March. She was fourteen this year.'

'Me too,' said Melanie. 'And you dinna get two lion tamers in the one circus, no more than you get two circuses in the one town. And I'm dead sure Papa didn't have a brother, neither. Only this sister, Tante Sylvie, sold the tickets. She liked to talk. She'd have said.'

'Then we'll rule that out,' said Mum. 'Now, about your not being twins. This is something Janice told me in confidence, but I think Melanie has a right to know.'

'Shall I clear off for a bit?' I said.

Mum hesitated.

'I don't think Janice has told Melly,' she said. 'I

28

don't know . . . It'll probably be simpler . . . Just don't talk about it to anyone. Is that all right with you, Melanie?'

'Course it is,' she said.

'Well,' said Mum. 'I don't know if Keith told you that his father died last October.'

'I think maybe I was at the funeral,' said Melanie. 'It was pissing down and everyone had their brollies up and I cried like I was never going to stop.'

'Oh, God . . .' said Mum. 'Sorry . . . I'll be all right in a moment . . . Can you spare me a cigarette?'

They both lit up and Mum took a puff or two and stubbed hers out and tried again.

'I suppose we'll get used to this,' she said, 'but there's something very uncomfortable about it . . . Well, I had a bad time after Mike died. Keith will tell you. I really went to pieces. I spent a lot of time weeping on people's shoulders, and of course Janice was one of them. I gather Keith's told you about Janice, so you'll have got it that she's rather . . . well, uptight and controlled, and perhaps not very good at emotions.'

'Keith tell you I thought you had to be my ma?' said Melanie. 'She wasn't my idea of a ma, the other one.'

'She's been a very good friend to me, though,' said Mum. 'She's the sort who sticks at it. A stupid emotional female sobbing her heart out over the coffee-biscuits isn't her scene at all, but she must have read up what to do, and talked to professionals, and somehow I think she got the idea that it

29

might be a help if she told me about something dreadful in her own life. So one evening she took a deep breath and screwed herself up and told me about what happened when Melly was born. She was twenty, and she was on a cycling holiday in the south of France with a couple of girlfriends, and one evening they were riding along – late, because they'd had a puncture that wouldn't mend – when they came across this circus camped out in the middle of nowhere, so they asked if they could put up their tent alongside them. They got chatting, and one of Janice's friends decided she fancied one of the acrobats, so they spent the rest of their holiday zigzagging around so as to meet up with the circus as often as possible. By the end of it they'd made quite a few friends in the circus, and they went home thinking they'd had an amusing holiday and that was it.

'So Janice just wasn't ready for it when a couple of weeks later she got a formal proposal of marriage from the lion tamer. The extraordinary thing, she said, was that she didn't think twice about it. As soon as she got over her surprise she knew she was going to say yes. It wasn't that she'd secretly fallen in love with him, or anything. Several of the men had tried to get off with her, and one of her English friends had slept around a bit, but the lion tamer had been formal and gallant and serious, and he didn't speak much English, either. But Janice had found him rather attractive in his odd way, and after last night I can see why. Besides, winter was settling in, and the relationship she'd had for a couple of years had come apart that summer, and she was hating her job, so she went back to Arles and married him.

'She must have been crazy, she told me. It didn't work out at all. She didn't understand circus life, and the other circus people treated her now as an outsider, and her husband was madly jealous if he saw her say even a couple of words to another man, and he had an appalling temper. He didn't actually beat her, but when he got into one of his rages he could be absolutely terrifying.'

'That's right,' said Melanie. 'Fact, it's better when he gets to hitting you. Annie's got him sorted, mind. She won't stand for any of that.'

'On top of that, he was a Catholic,' said Mum, 'and he wouldn't have any truck with contraception. Janice did her best not to get pregnant, but of course it happened in the end. As soon as he knew she was carrying his child he became very kind and considerate, and she thought it might be all right after all. And then the baby was born, a little girl, and he insisted on calling her Melanie, after his mother. He adored her. In fact, from what Janice told me, he was pretty well obsessed with her. He wanted to do everything for her himself. He even resented the fact that Janice could breastfeed her and he couldn't . . .'

'I'll buy that,' said Melanie. 'That's Papa.'

'Yes, I got a bit of that impression last night,' said Mum. 'Anyway, for Janice life became even worse than it had been before. Her husband didn't just revert to being madly jealous. He had this great ogress of a sister, and they both had desperately primitive ideas about child-rearing, really dangerous and unhygienic, some of them, but if she stepped out of line in the smallest detail they'd scream at her that she was trying to kill his child, and it wasn't long before Janice began to suspect that the sister was working on him to take the baby away from her and give it to one of the circus women to look after.

'So she decided to leave him. She'd got a little necklace and a bracelet and some other things which she sold secretly, and bought a railway ticket, and just as the circus was getting going one evening she slipped away with the baby. It was a local train and it took her only about twenty miles back to Arles. There wasn't a train out until the morning and she knew he'd come after her so she went and hid in a little hotel in a back street, but somehow he found out where she was, because in the middle of the night he came to her room with half a dozen other circus people. When she started to scream they put a gag in her mouth and tied her up and took the baby away, but two of them stayed with her all next day. After a bit they untied her and took the gag out, but they told her that if she made a noise they'd use it again. Apart from that they wouldn't say a word to her. They offered her food but she was too frantic to eat. They stayed with her all next night, but next morning her husband's sister came and gave the baby back. The other two left, but the sister gave her some money and said, "If you try to find my brother again your child will die. That is the truth. Now, go." In case you're thinking it might have been some other baby they'd found somewhere, it wasn't. You know your child after the first half hour.'

'Different babies wouldn't look the same now,' I said.

We sat and tried to think about it. Melanie stubbed out her fag and blew out a long smoky breath and stood up and stretched. As she did so the sleeve of her cardigan slid up, so that I saw, halfway up the forearm on the inside, a white scar like an inside-out N. I grabbed her by the wrist and showed Mum.

'I don't know how much more of this I can take,' said Mum.

'What's up?' said Melanie. 'Oh, that. Caught it on a nail one time we were loading the ponies. Papa was making me learn bareback.'

'Only Melly's is on her left arm, isn't it?' said Mum. 'You're right-handed, aren't you, Melanie? I noticed when you were lighting your cigarette just now.'

'Right as right,' said Melanie. 'Melly's left, is she? Mirror images, then? Don't you get that with twins?'

'Not always, I think,' said Mum. 'And anyway, those scars . . . What's more, Melly caught her arm on a nail at some stables where she was having

33

riding lessons. This is making me feel most peculiar.'

'Did Monsieur Perrault say anything to you about why he left the circus, Mum?' I asked. 'I mean, if he was making Melanie learn bareback he must have been expecting to stay on.'

'As a matter of fact he was rather odd about that,' said Mum. 'I remember Janice saying that one of her problems was that he adored his lions . . .'

'That's right,' said Melanie. 'He was nuts about them, and if one of them got ill . . . Always getting sick with something, lions.'

'But he was very offhand about them last night,' said Mum. 'It seems there was some sort of disagreement in the circus, but I'd have thought he'd have taken his lions off to some other circus, rather than giving it all up and moving to Edinburgh. It's almost as if he wanted to get as far away as possible . . . Look, I've got to go. I think the first thing is for me to try and ring Janice. No, hell, she's at a conference this weekend. She'll be home this evening. I'll try and . . . No, I can't – it's *Giovanni* and that goes on for ever. Maybe I can find a gap. Please, please, be careful, Melanie. It isn't just your father. There's something going on here . . . And you and Keith have got to work out a way of staying in touch.'

She was standing up by now.

'I'm really concerned about this,' she said. 'You were right in a way, Melanie. I do think of Melly as almost my own daughter.'

'Do I get in on that?' said Melanie, not joking, or not much.

Mum looked really pleased, but a notch more and she might have been crying.

'If this crazy business is true, you're in already,' she said. 'I'll see you at the theatre, darling. I might be clear by one.'

'I'll be there,' I said.

When Mum had gone we just sat there, not saying anything. I was thinking about Mum. It was a crazy business, like she'd said, but it had really done something for her. I hadn't seen her so alive, so interested, since my dad died. Suited me, anyway. If she actually wanted me to keep in touch with Melanie . . .

'He took me away from my own mother,' said Melanie, quietly, to herself, to nobody, to the world. She looked down at her arm and stroked the scar with her fingertip.

'And now we're being pushed around, I'm thinking. Yon's more than a wee coincidence, Keith. And it was more than a wee coincidence you happening down the stair just as I was happening up.'

'Your dad's doing it somehow, you mean?' I said.

She shook her head.

'No. I'm thinking it's like your ma was saying – maybe he came to Edinburgh to get as far away as possible. And maybe now there's something come after us . . . It'll be all about what he did when he took me away from my ma, when I was a wee bairn.'

She was dead serious, but it didn't make any sense to me.

'It's got to be something to do with the circus,' I said. 'They were all in it together. I don't believe in magic and stuff. I always knew Father Christmas was just a story.'

'This is no Father Christmas, Keith, but you'd best start believing in it.'

'If you say so . . . Well, supposing I did believe, I'd still say it was something to do with the circus. Was the circus just animals and acrobats and clowns, or was there something else? Palmists, I suppose, and fortune-tellers and stuff. They make out they do magic, sort of. You must have had some of that.'

'Just Madame Raquel,' she said. 'Herbs and potions, she sold, and she'd a crystal ball she looked in, but that was only, like, advertising for the potions. Herself, she'd tell you that, though she made a hocus-pocus of it for the customers. Buy me another Coke, then?'

'If you like.'

We wandered off and found a place where we settled down.

'Tell you what,' I said. 'We haven't got a holiday fixed for this year – Mum didn't have the heart. I could try and talk her into taking us out to Arles, see if I can find anything out.'

'They'll never talk to you.'

'What about you coming along too?'

'Don't be thick. And it's not just Papa – we get wall-to-wall tourists here, August. I'll be working my arse off in the restaurant.'

'Suppose . . .'

'It'd give me the creeps, besides.'

I looked at her because she'd said it in an odd way, more to herself than me.

'What do you mean?' I said.

'I dinna ken,' she said. 'Just sometimes I'm dreaming about it, and it's always bad.'

'That figures,' I said. 'Is this something new? Have you always had these dreams? When did they start? After you left, or before?'

'On the train it was, and very, very bad. It wasn't the whole dream then, only the flying. When it's the whole dream, I'm in the circus and I'm watching Papa feed the lions, and then a body comes – I don't see who it is – and he tells me he's going to feed his animal and I can watch if I've the fancy to, so I start off with him across this big open field, and there's one of the travelling cages way over on the other side. And then it comes into my mind that this fellow's planning to feed me to his animal, and he's a bit ahead of me and I turn and tiptoe away, and then I'm flying. I can see Papa far down below, waving to me, but I'm flying away, free as a bird. It's beautiful, Keith. But then I feel something following after me. It can't fly, but it's down there, following, calling for me, waiting until I am tired with flying. And then I'm getting heavy, and I ken that I can't fly much longer . . . and that's when I wake up. There's nobody I've told that to before, Keith. Nobody ever.'

'Melly has nightmares. I heard her having a bad

37

one, once, at Penmaenan. That was about flying, I think. She didn't want to talk about it.'

'No, she wouldn't.'

'Was there anything in the circus you were particularly afraid of? Your dad's lions, for instance?'

'Not they. I was feared of Tante Sylvie, of course, but so were all the others. A great ogress, your ma called her, and that's about right. Even Papa was feared of her. And one of the clowns, Monsieur Albert, I dinna ken why, since I'd nothing to do with him. The kids said he was a miser, and if you looked out in the wee small hours you'd see the light in his caravan, where he was sitting up late counting his gold. And Madame Zazu, who rode the bareback. Most days she'd be fine, but then the devil would be in her . . . When I was a bairn I heard a body say, "Keep away from Zazu, the devil's in her today," and I went and looked and I could see it glaring out of her eyes . . .'

'Run herself short of smack or something?'

'Maybe. But I kenned that Papa wouldn't let anybody touch me, and there was nothing to be feared of. Only him.'

We talked around and around until it was time for her to go back to Annie's. She'd told Monsieur Perrault she was meeting me, so it was all right for me to go along with her. On the way I bought a bunch of flowers for Annie, to say thank you for last night's dinner. I started to bother about what Melanie might be thinking of me. I'd got the feeling she liked talking to me, but I was pretty sure I'd be a lot younger, and a lot less streetwise, than the sort of boy she usually hung around with.

I glanced at her, trying to guess what she felt, but she wasn't noticing me at all. I could tell that at once. We were almost at Annie's by now, and she was walking along looking calm and sure and set. I'd seen exactly that look before once, on Melly, when she'd dealt with the yellow dog. The lion tamer's daughter.

Mum was almost through when I got to the theatre, so she took me out to a not-bad vegetarian place for lunch. The business with Melly and Melanie had really got a grip on her. She'd obviously been thinking about it pretty well solidly since she'd left us.

'I've had a thought,' she said. 'It's almost too crazy to mention, but so's the whole business.'

'Except that it's happening,' I said. 'It's all right, Mum. I won't stomp on you. I've been swapping crazy stuff with Melanie all morning.'

(I'd better explain that Mum and Dad used to argue about this sort of thing. Crop circles, for instance. Mum said they meant something and I said they were made by hoaxers, and Dad said they were made by people who *thought* they were hoaxers but were really under the control of little green people from Alpha Centauri.)

'Well,' she said. 'Do you know what a *doppelgänger* is? We did a play about one four years ago at the Other Place. It was by one of those gloomy old Germans, very intense and poetical and utterly boring, I thought, but the point was that the hero had this double who seemed to be some kind of fiend, who stalked him, and if ever they came face to face the hero was going to die. I think the idea came from an old German fairy story . . . I know it sounds stupid as soon as I say it, but do you remember what Melly's aunt said when she gave the baby back? I'd assumed it was just a threat, that her brother would kill Melly if Janice tried to get in touch with him, or the aunt would, or something, but if you think about the *doppelgänger* story . . . I mean, I've never understood why the aunt brought the baby back, after Monsieur Perrault had taken all that trouble to get hold of her. Janice's explanation is that he was under his sister's thumb, and the sister wanted Janice out of their lives, and she knew that as long as they'd got the baby Janice wouldn't stop trying to get her back, so she bullied him into giving her up.'

'I'd go along with that. Melanie said everyone was frightened of her aunt, including Monsieur Perrault.'

'But then where did Melanie come from?'

'I don't know. And you're not going to tell me either of them's any kind of fiend. Or that Melly's the real Melly and Melanie's her doppelthingy. I'm not having that. They're both just as real as you or me.'

'You don't have to shout, darling. I completely agree with you about that. If you'd brought Melanie home out of the blue one evening and she'd not been Melly's double and so on, then I don't say

I wouldn't have been a bit alarmed for you, but as things are I feel just as concerned for her as I do for Melly. In fact, though I've met her just twice, I feel as if I've known her for most of her life. I want you to do something for me, darling. You're going to think it's stupid, but I have a very strong feeling it's important. It's the sort of feeling I've learnt to trust. Are you going to be talking to Melanie again soon?'

'She's ringing me at home tomorrow. After school. Is it all right if I ring off and call her back, so that it's on our bill?'

'Yes, of course. And when you're talking to her I want you to try to persuade her not to get in touch with Melly for the moment. Melly's staying with Christine . . .' (that's a friend of Janice's and Mum's in Coventry) '. . . but she'll be home this evening. I want you to ring her too . . .'

'I was going to, anyway, and tell her about Melanie.'

'Yes, of course. Then will you say the same to her, about not getting in touch? Try and get them to take it seriously, darling, even if you don't believe in it yourself.'

'Look, Mum. I take *you* seriously. I believe in you.'

That shook her. It shook me too. It's not the sort of thing you say.

'Do you want me to tell them about the dop-pelthingies?' I said, to cover it up.

'*Doppelgänger*s. Um . . . I think not . . . There's no point in frightening them . . .'

41

'It's all right. I'll just say you've got a bad feeling about it. They'd probably pay more attention to that than anything, anyway. Both of them. Melanie thinks you're terrific, you know. I'm hoping she'll put up with me because it gives her an in to you.'

'I'm glad you're having fun, darling.'

None of this worked out. I took the coach to Glasgow after lunch and got out to Bearsden somewhere around six o'clock. I went home first to see to the cats and check the post and the answerphone. There was only one message, from Melly, saying she'd be home by three and would I call her as soon as poss, so I made myself a mug of tea and dialled her number. She answered first ring, and as soon as she heard my voice she broke in.

'Who were you talking to this morning? You met them yesterday on some steps and you went to a caff and drank Coke and talked and talked, and then you ran and got into a taxi, I think, and then . . . no, I'll leave that bit out . . . there was a restaurant. And a man and a woman. Some sort of fuss going on. No. Wait. Yesterday evening you came back to the restaurant with Trish and had what looked like a really nice meal, and champagne, and the man and the woman were there again, and the man was sitting and talking and talking to Trish, and she was playing up to him. I think they were talking French. And somebody . . . somebody brought you the meal and did the waiting and so on . . . This is all real, isn't it? I'm not making it up. Tell me I'm not making it up.'

She was pretty upset, I could hear.

'You're not making it up,' I said. 'It all happened. The bit you left out was looking at your own face in a wing mirror, wasn't it?'

'And rubbing some dirt in. Who is she, Keith? What's her name?'

'Melanie Perrault. We think she's your twin, only Mum says she can't be.'

'And the man's my father, then?'

'Looks as though he's got to be.'

'I thought so. Oh, God! Tell Trish to watch out for him, Keith. He's got a foul temper. What's she like, then? Does she call herself Melly too?'

'No. Melanie. Suppose you smoked a bit and swore a bit and had your hair cut ragged . . . You remember that picture you drew of how you'd get yourself up if Janice would let you? That's what she was wearing – it looks as if you'd actually seen her trying it on in the shop. But the clothes and the hair don't matter . . . Jesus, was I glad to see you coming up those steps. Notice how I stared?'

'Did I notice? A right twit you looked, Keith.'

'Thanks. OK, I'll go on from there . . .'

I settled down and did that, best I could remember, backtracking when I'd left anything out. It must have taken getting on an hour – but at least Sundays were cheap-rate.

'How long has this been going on?' I asked her when I'd finished. 'It's when you get those dopey fits, isn't it? You've had them ever since I've known you.'

43

'Always,' she said. 'But not like this before. It was just bits, and I knew it wasn't real. I mean I knew I was sitting at the kitchen table or somewhere – I mean like when you're watching TV, you can get very involved, but you know it isn't happening to you, really. This time it almost was.'

'Except you couldn't hear what we were saying?'

'I can sometimes, but only when I'm not trying. It drives me crazy. You know when you're reading a book in a dream and you're getting along fine until you start paying attention, and then the words won't stay still any more. It's always been like that. When I was little, and still when I was in junior school for a bit, it used to be in some kind of circus, and I knew it was in France because sometimes I'd hear them talking French, and I'd understand what they were saying although my French wasn't really that good, but as soon as I tried to listen it didn't make any sense at all. And last night I could hear that Trish and the man were talking French but I was trying to listen to you and it was just a sort of jumble.'

'We were talking about Hole and P. J. Harvey, if you want to know. Do you have nightmares about a man leading you across a field towards a sort of circus trailer, and then you running away and finding you can fly, only something's pulling you down, following you below? . . . Melly? . . . Are you there?'

'She has that too?' she whispered. 'Look, I've got to talk to her. What's her number?'

I wasn't ready. I was still trying to think what to say when she said, 'No, that's no good. I can't call her at the restaurant because of him. I don't suppose you gave her my number.'

'No, but . . .'

'Then what's her address? Hell, I bet he opens her letters. She's calling you up tomorrow, isn't she? Hell, I can't wait till tomorrow . . .'

By now I was getting scared. It wasn't what she was saying, it was the way she was saying it, right over the top with excitement. Melly wasn't like that.

'Hold it,' I said. 'Mum doesn't think it's a good idea, you two getting in touch. She told me to tell you.'

'Oh, come off it – that's just Trish. Anyway, we've just got to . . .'

'Listen,' I said. 'Can't you at least wait till Janice gets home? She can talk to Trish. I'll give you her number . . .'

'Oh, great! She's still in Edinburgh! She can get a message round, can't she? I'll call her!'

'She's working tonight, Melly. She's at the theatre. No! For God's sake, listen! Mum's working, and you can't ring her there. She'll be back in her hotel room – hell, the show's a long one, she said – about half-past eleven. You wait till Janice gets home, and tell her all about it, and then one of you can call Mum tonight, if you still want to. If Janice wants to talk to me, I'll be round at Ken's. The number's on that card I sent you. And Mum's going to call her tomorrow evening anyway. Got a pencil? Here's Mum's number.'

I gave it her and tried to calm her down a bit but it wasn't any use so we rang off and I fed the cats and went round to Ken's. Nobody called me there. I was exhausted, but I didn't sleep that well. The way Melly had talked had really upset me.

Next morning at school I went to the library to get Mrs McCrum to help me look up about *doppelgänger*s. I still felt it was a crazy notion but at least it was something I could do. Mrs McCrum likes kids using the library for their own stuff, and on top of that she's a fantasy nut, so she dug around and found some bits and pieces, but there wasn't much and they all said the same sort of thing about German folk tales and gloomy German and Russian writers. Some of the stories said that *doppelgänger*s were the ghosts of living people, haunting them, and some of them said they were fiends out to get them, but either way if you met yours it meant you were going to die, or else it happened straight off. There wasn't anything about where they came from, or it being two real people like Melly and Melanie.

When I got home to do the cats that evening I found Melanie sitting huddled in the porch. She was wearing the gear I'd first seen her in, and looked totally done in, but all the same she was fizzing. Before I could say anything she jumped up and said, 'I've effed things up, Keith. Real bad. You've got to help. She's here. We're both here and we can't get her back. Listen. I was in my room and having one of my fits, real strong, just yakking and yakking into the telephone. I kenned well she must be talking with you but I couldna hear the words, only the buzz of it going through me till I was shuddering with it. I thought I was going to fly to pieces. I couldn't bear for you to be talking with her and me so far off. I was screaming for you both to stop so I could talk to her myself. There's a phone in Annie's own room. It's another number from the restaurant. I pushed the fit aside and called Enquiries and asked them for Perraults living in Coventry. J, I told them, and there was only the one. As soon as I saw you were finished I called that number, and she answered and said, 'Hi,' but before I could say an effing word myself she was there, with me, in Annie's room above the restaurant. Wait . . .'

She'd been gabbling away a hundred miles an hour while I got the door unlocked and took her into the kitchen. Now she shut her eyes and concentrated a moment and opened them and said, 'I'm sorry, Keith. But I couldn't help it. It was too strong for me, and now I can't get back.'

It was Melly's voice, exactly.

'Jesus!' I said. 'What's happened to the rest of you?'

'I don't know,' she said. 'This isn't right, Keith, not like this. There's still two of us . . . Where's Trish?'

'She'll be at the theatre now. I can't ring her there.'

Automatically I went on with putting the kettle

47

on and getting the teapot out. I fished Melly's mug out of the back of the cupboard and put it on the table. She grabbed it and sort of fondled it as if it was some kind of magic charm which would get her out of this.

'What happened next?' I said. 'How did you make it here?'

It was Melanie who answered. She didn't sound quite so off the handle, now that she'd got the mug in her hands.

'Papa came up, yelling at me for being late down, but I was near crazed myself and I began yelling right back at him for what he'd done with me when I was a wee bairn, and when he got what I was saying he really lost it. I thought he would have killed me but Annie heard the racket and came up and tried to stop him. She couldn't hold him but I got to the door and ran down, and she must have clung on to him somehow and I was out in the street and away. I had no money. I thought of looking for your ma, but I didna ken if she'd told him she was working in the theatre, and maybe he'd come for me there. Then I poked in my pocket and found the paper where you'd written your address and I thought I'd try that. I dossed out, and in the morning I bummed myself a cut of bread and walked all the way to the motorway, where the hitchers hang out, and I found a fellow and a girl to hitch along with into Glasgow. I was asking my way to Bearsden, saying I'd lost my purse, and a woman gave me the money for the bus. I'd heard you saying to your ma about feeding your cats, so I kenned you'd be by. But Keith, I'm effing hungry.'

'I'll fix you some scrambled eggs. That's what Melly . . . hell, I suppose you know that. For God's sake which of you is it in there?'

I was watching her do exactly what Melly would have done about her tea. First, a great splosh of milk into the mug, and then a fiddling little half-spoon of sugar, tipped slowly in as if she was trying to count the grains, and then stir and stir until the tea was ready to pour.

'There's the two of us, buzzing against each other,' said Melanie's voice, 'and there isn't room for us both. We can't go on like this, Keith, or we'll be flying apart.'

'I believe you,' I said. Anyone would have spotted there was something wrong. She was obviously on a high, but it was a sick sort of high, spiky, edgy, dangerous-feeling. Her eyes glittered and her whole body seemed tense and twanging. She clung to her mug as if it was all that was keeping her from flying to pieces, like she'd said. I didn't know what to do. It wasn't any use calling a doctor. I couldn't ring Mum at the theatre . . . well, I could try, if it was this important . . . Or Janice – she probably wouldn't be home, but it was worth a go . . .

I put the teapot on the table and gave Melanie her eggs. I was waiting for her to finish pouring so that I could have a cup when the telephone rang. It was Mum.

'Thank heavens you're there,' she said. 'I

haven't got much time, but something dreadful has happened. Janice called, early this afternoon. She got home last night and found Melly in a coma, and the telephone off the hook. She rushed her to hospital but they couldn't find anything wrong. She stayed with her all night and all this morning, until she'd talked to the doctors, and then she went home to pick up things for her. While she was there she noticed a number Melly had written on the telephone pad so she called it. She didn't know who'd be there, but there was a room number and they put it through to me. By the mercy of heaven I'd had the morning off and was just getting ready to come round to the theatre. I was horrified when she told me what had happened, but all I could think of was that it might be something to do with Melanie, so I explained about all that. Janice didn't want to listen – it's not her sort of thing. I had to stop, because she was getting upset, and it wasn't until I'd rung off that I worked out you were the only person who could have given her my number. I'm stuck here now till the third act's started, and then I'm going to hare up to Annie's . . .'

'Don't do that,' I said. 'Listen. Did you tell Monsieur Perrault you were anything to do with the opera?'

'No. Why? I did tell him I made costumes, but he seemed to think I meant I was a dressmaker. He wasn't very interested in me. He wanted to talk about himself.'

'Thank God for that,' I said. 'I was afraid he might be coming after you.'

'After me? Why on earth?'

'Because Melanie had a row with him and cleared out. She's here. And so's Melly, sort of.'

'There? At Bearsden?'

I explained what had happened. She was wonderful. She just accepted it as if there wasn't anything crazy about it.

'This is dreadful,' she said when I'd finished. 'What on earth are we going to do?'

'The first thing I've got to do is try and get Melanie calmed down,' I said. 'She can't go on much longer like she is.'

'Try to get her to have a nice warm bath. Not too hot. You'll have to turn the water on and it'll take about an hour to get hot. I wonder if it would be safe to give her one of my tranquillizers. They're very mild. In the pink box in the drawer by my bed. Just one. I've got to go now, but—'

'Wait,' I said. 'Can you ring Maisie . . .' (that's Ken's mum) '. . . and tell her I won't be round tonight? Say I've got a friend come unexpected, and they're not very well, and I'm looking after them.'

'I'll fit that in somehow. Good luck, darling . . .'

'Hold it,' I said again, because Melanie had come out into the hallway, where our telephone is, and was making signs. I nodded to her to go ahead and butt in. It wasn't Melanie, though, it was Melly.

'Give her my love,' she said. 'And ask her where Mum is – I want to talk to her.'

I passed the message on. I think it shook Mum, and I can see why. It made Melly being in Bearsden real, somehow, in a way just talking about it hadn't.

'Sorry,' she said. 'She'll be at the hospital – Walsgrave. The number's in my old address book. On the shelf with the cookery books. And give her all my love back. And Melanie too. I've got to go now. Good luck, darling – I think you're doing wonders.'

We rang off. I turned the hot water on and found the pills and gave one to Melanie and told her what it was. She looked at it a moment.

'I dinna ken,' she said. 'Hell, we've got to try something – we're just about hanging on, only.'

I got through to the hospital but they absolutely refused to go and find Janice for me. I made it as urgent as I could, but my voice doesn't sound that grown-up and I got a bit upset, so I wasn't sure they'd taken me seriously. Then all we could do was wait. It was only half an hour, but it was for ever.

'Hold me tight,' said Melanie suddenly. 'Hold on to me, Keith!'

I took her into the lounge and turned the telly on and we sat on the sofa with my arms round her. That should have been fun but it wasn't. It was like holding a wild bird, one that's got into the house and you've caught it and you're carrying it out in your hand with its wings folded so it can't flap them and hurt itself, and it lies there still and quivering – like that.

And then the telephone rang and I let go and she flew to it like the bird.

I went into the kitchen but left the door open so that I could see out into the hallway, so I could check she was OK without listening in. She'd settled down on the chair with the handset in the nook of her shoulder, the way she always does, because she can't help doing body language with her hands even when the other person can't see. She did most of the talking, and cried a bit, but it didn't make any difference her being Melly now – she still had the same twanging, fizzing jumpiness pulsing out of her . . . And then, right in front of my eyes, she sort of slumped. The phone slid off her shoulder but she grabbed it and took a deep, slow breath and said something, and then held it out for me to come and take.

'She's gone,' she said in her Melanie voice. 'Tell her, Keith. I'm done for.'

I took the phone and said, 'Janice? This is me. Keith.'

'What now, for God's sake?' she said.

She sounded really upset.

'Melanie says Melly's gone. She was here. They were both in Melanie's body . . .'

'Are we all crazy?'

'No, we're not. *It's* crazy, but . . . I mean, weren't you talking to Melly just now? Didn't she tell you what had been happening?'

'Somebody I thought was Melly was telling me something I thought was a lot of nonsense, and I don't understand it and I'm extremely upset . . . wait . . . someone seems to be looking for me . . .'

I heard voices, then Janice again, crying as she spoke.

'I've got to go, Keith. I'm in the sister's office. That was the nurse. She says Melly's woken up and she's asking for me. I'll try and call you back.'

I went and told Melanie and then I pretty well collapsed, sitting at the kitchen table with my head in my hands, shuddering with relief.

After a bit Melanie said, 'That was an effing close thing, Keith. Christ, I'm shattered. Is there a fag anywhere?'

I found her a pack of Mum's, and an ashtray, and took her into the lounge where she slumped on the sofa. She hadn't finished her eggs, but they were cold, so I took a loaf out of the freezer and defrosted it in the microwave and made her a peanut butter and redcurrant jelly sandwich, which Melly had a craze for, and she wolfed it, so I made her another. When the water was hot I ran her a bath and pretty well forced her to go and get into it and while I was there I made up the spare bed, and then I put a message on the answerphone saying I'd be back in twenty minutes and went round to Ken's to tell Maisie I really was all right, and to borrow some milk – we'd used up what I'd got for the cats.

When I got back I found Melanie had fallen asleep in the bath and I had to yell at her to wake her up. She got out, grumbling and swearing, and dried herself, sort of, and staggered out in the pyjamas I'd given her, tripping over the trouser ends. I pushed her into bed and tucked her in and turned the light out. When I said goodnight she didn't answer.

Now there wasn't anything to do except fix myself something to eat and wait for Janice to call and worry about how I could skip school next day, let alone the rest of the week until the opera finished in Edinburgh. Janice did ring in the end. She was still upset, but differently. She said Melly was OK as far as anyone could make out, but they were keeping her in hospital for observation. And she'd told Janice everything she'd done since the phone call – everything Melanie had done, that is – being beaten up by Monsieur Perrault, and getting away, and sleeping out, and hitching over to Glasgow and finding our place and waiting for me to get home, the lot. It was the bit about Monsieur Perrault that convinced Janice. He'd been her husband, remember, but Melly couldn't possibly have known what he was like.

'I absolutely hate this,' she told me. 'I find it extremely stupid and extremely frightening, and I think I'd rather we were all crazy. But I have to accept that it's happening.'

I told her I felt the same, and asked her to give my love to Melly. I said I'd ring Mum and tell her what had happened.

In fact Mum rang me from the theatre during the last act. I could hear the singers shrieking and bellowing away in the background. I said it looked as if Melly had got back somehow, and she was out of her coma and so on. I asked her to call my school and tell them I wouldn't be in because I wasn't feeling too good – and what about the rest of the week? She told me she'd talked to the Alicia person who'd come in to help with the costume crisis and she was going to take over from tomorrow, but Mum would have to go in in the morning to show her the ropes, and she should be home by teatime. Was I relieved! I flopped into bed and slept till the middle of the morning, when the telephone rang. It was Janice, saying Melly seemed pretty well normal and the hospital were letting her go home. I told her about Mum, and fixed that they'd talk that evening.

Melanie was still asleep, but she looked OK and was breathing easy. I had some Weetabix and was grilling bacon when she groped her way into the kitchen, all woozy and pathetic in my old dressing gown.

'That smells effing good,' she said. 'Do some for me?'

I told her about Janice and Melly. I wanted to talk about what had happened so that we'd know what to do next time. I mean, was it the tranquillizer, or talking to Janice, or something just snapping? I thought this was important, but Melanie wasn't that interested.

'Next time we're stuck with it,' she said. 'So it's effing well got not to happen.'

We got dressed and watched idiot afternoon TV, and a video, and I went out and bought stuff for supper. I was almost at our road when I saw Ken coming along from the other direction, so I walked on and met up with him. He was on his way round to our place to tell me about this bird he'd seen at the weekend which might have been something crazily rare but was probably just an albino blackbird. I said I couldn't ask him back in as our friend who wasn't well was asleep now and I didn't want to disturb her. It worked out OK, but it made me realize we'd got to have a story about Melanie. We'd got to have something for her to do, and we couldn't leave her alone in the house all day, either. It wasn't just that she'd have gone crazy with boredom – she didn't feel as if it was safe to leave her alone that long.

When I got home Mum was there, so of course we started talking the whole thing through again.

'At least it's taught us a lesson,' Mum said. 'We don't understand what we're dealing with, but we know from now on that we've got to be extremely careful. You aren't going to try calling Melly again, are you?'

'Course not,' said Melanie, 'and neither's she – but it's going to be effing hard. Sorry, Trish. But you don't understand. Nobody can understand but us. We're each calling the other, calling and calling . . . When Keith was away just now, and before you were home, it swept over me till I was screaming inside me, shaking and sweating and holding myself down so that I didn't go running off to hitch my way to Coventry. And the same with her, and that isn't guessing. It's a thing I ken. But I dinna ken how long I can take it.'

'It isn't like when you're having one of your dopey fits?' I said.

'No, nothing like. That was before I kenned for sure she was real, and in a place I could be going to – I could walk into a room and she'd be there, waiting for me. Before, I was only watching, seeing what she was seeing, and she'd not have kenned I was there. Now I can feel her. Put a cloth over my eyes and spin me round, and I'll point you where she is. I could walk straight to her, and maybe I'd weary on the way and fall asleep, but my body would go on walking to her.'

Then the phone rang and I went to answer it. It was Janice.

'Melly thinks this is safe,' she said. 'I hope to heavens she's right. Is Trish back yet? Can I talk to her?'

Mum came and I went back into the kitchen. In spite of what Melly had told Janice I was pretty anxious. I thought any sort of connection between where the two girls were might make something happen, but when I asked Melanie she shook her head.

'It isn't that way,' she said. 'Just now I ken with my mind she's there, and that's our ma talking with Trish, and that's it. It's the other times, when the whole of me's aching and screaming for us to be together, body and soul, just the one body, just the one soul . . . Mary, mother of God, help me!'

She wasn't swearing either, she was praying. I'd never heard anyone do that before, not for real.

I took hold of her hand and held it and she started to cry, quietly, wiping the tears away with her sleeve and swearing under her breath and crying again. This is going to sound really stupid, but I was glad she was doing it. She needed to cry, and she needed to hold my hand so that she could do it, and she trusted me enough to let herself go like that. Yes, I was glad.

The next few days were a real muddle. I'm not going to write down all the different telephone calls and so on, mostly Mum and Janice, but sometimes me talking to Melly and sometimes Melanie and Janice trying to get to know each other a bit. It was specially hard on Janice, Mum said, getting used to the idea that there was this other daughter, or other half of one daughter, depending how you looked at it, who she'd never met and who'd lived this life she didn't know anything about. And on top of that, Janice still hated the idea that there wasn't some kind of ordinary, real-world explanation for what had happened. That's why I put in that bit about the other daughter or the half-daughter. Melanie and Melly were absolutely set, certain, sure that they were two halves who'd somehow come apart, but Janice was just as certain they were two different people, and always had been and always would be, and what was happening between them was some kind of psychic freak.

'She thinks she might have had twins without knowing it,' Mum said. 'She had a perfectly appalling labour, in their caravan, with the horrible sister and a couple of old hags from the circus acting as midwives. It was extremely primitive and full of superstitious nonsense, and she passed out several times, so I suppose it's just possible. I know in some places people are very superstitious about twins, because they think one of them must have come from the devil, though I've never heard of that happening in France. But I can tell you one thing – the little boy I was looking after when I was an au pair was perfectly obviously left-handed, but when I suggested he might be, the family was very upset, and the grandmother wanted the parents to sack me on the spot. There'd never been the slightest taint of left-handedness in either family, she said. So what Janice thinks now – or rather what she seems to be trying to persuade herself – is that she had twins without knowing it and they took the left-handed one away . . .'

'You said there didn't have to be a left-handed one,' I said.

'No, I don't think so, and I wouldn't have thought you could tell that small. But these are very superstitous people and perhaps they believed they could. Anyway, let me go on . . . Then, when she ran away with the baby and they came after her and took it away, what they did was exchange it for the other one, which they'd farmed out somewhere, and bring that one back. I must say I don't believe that either. You know your baby and it knows you, however like the new one might be, though according to Janice it cried and cried and wouldn't stop for days after they brought it back.'

'But you dinna believe it,' said Melanie. 'Tell me you dinna believe it, Trish. It's—'

She was trying not to swear when Mum was around, and sometimes it was pretty funny when she bit something back at the last moment, but not now. She was really upset.

'No, I don't,' said Mum. 'I can believe in somebody having twins and not realizing it, in circumstances like that, but not in people discovering at once that one of them was left-handed . . .'

'They didn't have to know then,' I said. 'They could just believe one of them was going to be, and take the second one away and keep it until they found out, and then do the swap. And they were just about ready to do that when Janice cleared out, so they had to come after her. And you did say the baby cried a lot, after.'

I could have kicked myself. I'd only just registered that Melanie really couldn't cope with Janice's kind of explanation, about twins and so on, and I needn't have blurted that out, even if it made a sort of sense. Anyway, Melanie totally lost it.

'That's crap!' she yelled. 'I tell you it's effing crap! We're one! I'm her and she's me, and the eff with anything else!'

'I believe you,' said Mum. 'You know it's so and Melly knows it's so, and that's all the argument I need. What Keith said was perfectly sensible, but what's happening isn't sensible.'

61

'We canna go on this way,' said Melanie. 'I tell you, we canna go on this way!'

Another evening I was doing homework in the kitchen (you get a lot of that in Scottish schools), Mum was at the theatre and Melanie was in the lounge watching TV. I was steaming along through some maths when she yelled at me to come and see. I yelled back I was busy and she came rushing out and started trying to pull me out of my chair, yelling at me it was important and I'd got to come. I could see she was on one of her highs so I said I'd come for a bit.

It was a programme about Siamese twins. There'd been stuff in the news about a pair who'd been born in Liverpool that they were going to try and separate, and this was some kind of documentary about other pairs. It wasn't my sort of thing. Given the chance I'd have zapped to another channel, but Melanie made me watch the lot. Some of the twins hadn't got a chance. They'd got shared livers and kidneys and things, and there was no way they could be cut apart and both of them live. The ones who were more lightly joined the surgeons could do something about, but it was always chancy. We were looking at a pair who were joined at the chest when Melanie pressed the mute button.

'That's us,' she said. 'That's me and Melly.'

I stared at the screen. They were babies still, about a year old, I guessed. Two heads, four arms, four legs, and this body thing in the middle. It was a still photograph, not film. Both faces were screwed up, both mouths seemed to be crying, all eight limbs struggled and threshed. It was horrible.

'They canna live like that,' said Melanie, 'and you canna cut them free of each other.'

She always sounded much more Scottish when she was upset. After a bit she pressed the button again.

'. . . Died at two and a half years,' said the voice-over. 'Even with modern surgical techniques, it is unlikely that either of them would have survived an operation to separate them.'

She didn't say anything else until the programme was over and she'd switched off.

'Do you see now, Keith?' she said. 'It isna livers and that we share, but try and make us two, the way you and my ma are trying, and one of us will be dead. Both of us, very like. We must be one, like we were when we were born. We must be *made* one.'

'Made one? How?'

'I dinna ken. All I ken is when I was a wee bairn I was one, and Papa took me away and made me two, and one he gave back to my ma and one he kept for himself, but we couldna live long like that, no more than the bairns in the programme. I tell you this, Keith. If you hadna been coming down the steps by Princes Street the morning you were, there'd have been some other thing happen to pull us together again.'

'What would happen if you just met, and got it over with?'

'The one of us would be dead, and the other would go crazy past curing.'

I'd never said anything to her about *doppel-gängers*, and nor had anyone else as far as I knew. I didn't bother to ask how she could be so sure. She wouldn't have been able to tell me.

When Mum came home she called Janice, which she did most evenings. Janice said that Melly hadn't watched the TV programme, but she'd described the Siamese twins to her and said almost exactly the same things that Melanie had been saying to me.

I had three weeks back at school after Edinburgh, before the summer holidays started, so we had to work out what to do about Melanie. We couldn't risk leaving her alone. She said so too. I'd be doing homework and she'd be listening to a tape on my Walkman and she'd jerk up and stare in front of her. Or maybe she'd be watching TV in the lounge and she'd come sort of sleepwalking into the kitchen and mutter to me in a dead kind of voice, 'Hang on to me, Keith,' and I'd stop what I was doing and simply hold her tight, ten minutes, quarter of an hour sometimes, and she'd give a big sigh and say, 'Ta, I'll do now,' and I'd let go. If anyone had come in and found us they'd have got the wrong idea. OK, I was keen on her in a way I'd never been on Melly, or anyone else come to that, but what was happening to her was too serious for that kind of messing around.

Janice couldn't leave Melly alone either, but that

wasn't as much of a problem, because Melly had school, and friends, and all her usual life to hang on to. Melanie didn't have any of that, nothing to anchor her down. Mum arranged to go in to the opera afternoons and evenings, and she took Melanie in with her to give her a hand. Then I'd take the bus in after school and bring Melanie back to Bearsden, though sometimes we hung around in Glasgow for a couple of hours so she could buy a few clothes and get to see a bit of life. Mum and I'd only been a few months in Bearsden, so people didn't know that much about us. Our story was that Melanie was half-French, and her mum was a friend of Mum's, but her parents had split up and she was staying with us while things got sorted out, and we were being careful in case her dad showed up and tried to take her away. That was all pretty well true; in fact I gave myself nightmares about Monsieur Perrault somehow nosing her out, the way he'd found Janice at the hotel when she'd run away from the circus. Luckily there are pages and pages of Robinsons in the Glasgow phone book. I suppose if he'd gone to the police about Melanie going missing, and told them it might have something to do with Mum, they'd have tracked us down, but Melanie said he wouldn't because he didn't trust policemen. We didn't see anything about her in the papers or on the local news.

Mum worked in the sewing room in the theatre, next door to what they called the Wardrobe, which was a big room stacked with racks of costumes and shelves of boots and hats and shoes and gloves and sword belts and so on for all the different productions. They'd have two or three operas on the go, and maybe a couple of others being got ready, and there might be fifty or sixty people in the cast, what with the chorus and everything. That's a lot of costumes.

Usually there'd be half a dozen women in the sewing room, stitching and cutting, but with the opera on tour it was just Mum in the evenings. I got there one time and found her sitting on a pile of clothes with Melanie on her lap, rocking her to and fro like a baby. They both looked utterly exhausted.

'Thank God you're here at last,' said Mum, though I wasn't late. 'I don't know what's up, but Melanie's been having a very bad time. I haven't sewn a stitch for the last two hours and I've a pile of work to do. Do you think you can take her home, darling? She seems to be quieter now. You'd better take a taxi. My wallet's in my jacket pocket. Will you be all right with Keith, Melanie? You can call me if it gets bad again and I'll come straight home.'

Melanie stood up, shivering. I could see she'd been crying.

'I'll do fine,' she muttered. 'Sorry about that, Trish. I couldn't stop myself.'

'That's all right,' said Mum. 'I could see you couldn't. I'm going to start sewing, but don't let Keith take you away till you're ready.'

'I'll do fine,' said Melanie again. 'I'll just be going to the toilet.'

66

As soon as she was out of the room I asked Mum what had happened.

'I'm not sure,' said Mum. 'I was sewing in here and Melanie had wandered out and after a bit I went to see where she'd got to – I can't help feeling anxious about her, you know. She'd wandered into the Wardrobe and she must have been trying on some of the costumes – she's done that before; I told her she could . . . Anyway I found her sort of stuck in front of the mirror – you know, the full-length one – wearing one of the green cloaks from *Trovatore* – far too big for her but just right for her colouring. I asked if she was all right and she didn't seem to hear me, so I asked a bit louder and she still didn't. But when I actually touched her she spun round and screamed, and stared at me as if I was some kind of wild animal. Next thing she was yelling and swearing. She didn't know me at all. And we had a rehearsal going on so all I could do was drag her in here and shut the door and try and get her calmed down. And that's what I've been doing ever since. I'm desperately behind, darling. I'm going to be late back – well after ten, I should think. Are you sure you can cope? You'll call if you need me, won't you? The receptionist's name is Mercy. She's much less of a dragon than she tries to sound. Anyway I'll warn her you may be calling . . .'

Then Melanie came back and said thank you and sorry again to Mum, and Mum gave her a hug and we left. I started looking for a taxi, but Melanie said she'd rather walk a bit. In the end we walked the whole way back to Bearsden, which is all of seven miles. We didn't talk much at first. I didn't want to bother her. We must have been nearly halfway home when she said, 'I was blowing around, Keith, blowing around this great cold empty space. Like . . . you've seen a paper bag blowing along a street on a windy day, high up between the buildings, whirling and jinking wherever the wind tells it? Like that. And you know what was in there with me? The creature, the one in the travelling cage, like I told you about in my nightmares. And there was this wee glass door I must get to, if ever I was to come out of that place. And I could see myself standing in my green cloak on the other side of the wee glass door . . . It wasn't any dream, Keith. It was the worst thing that has ever come to me in all my days.'

It was after half-past nine when we got home. Melanie had a bath while I fixed supper. She came down in her dressing gown and we ate off our knees in the lounge, watching the telly. Then I went into the kitchen to get on with my homework. After a bit I looked into the lounge to see if she was OK, and she was curled up asleep on the sofa, so I got a duvet and put it over her and went back to my homework. Somewhere around ten Janice rang and I told her Mum was still at the theatre.

'Well, will you tell her Christine has confirmed she can have Melly this weekend?' she said. 'So I'll definitely be coming up, late on Friday.'

(She'd been going to come the weekend before.

She was desperate to meet Melanie, of course. But at the last minute Christine had had something happen which meant she couldn't look after Melly, and there was no one else Janice felt it was safe to leave her with. I don't know what she'd told Christine – as much as she could without sounding crazy, I expect.)

'Great,' I said. 'I'll pass that on. I can't tell Melanie now because she's asleep . . . Is Melly OK?'

Janice hesitated. I guessed she'd sooner have talked to Mum about it. She's not as good as Mum is at letting me (or Melly, come to that) in on things.

'I think she's all right now,' she said. 'Why? Did something happen your end?'

I told her, except for what Melanie had told me. I feel that was private to Melanie.

'About what time would this have been?' said Janice.

I worked it out. Mum had said two hours.

'Around half-past three,' I said.

There was another pause while she made up her mind whether to tell me any more.

'I'd rather talk to Trish about it,' she said. 'I'm sorry, Keith, but it's all a bit private and personal. It's not that I don't trust you . . .'

'That's all right,' I said, though actually I felt pretty miffed – I'd told her about Melanie, hadn't I? 'Mum should be home about . . . oh, any minute now. I'll get her to call you, shall I?'

'If she's not too tired,' she said, and we rang off.

*

I told Mum when she got in, and she rang and talked for getting on an hour but I was still doing my homework when she finished so she came into the kitchen and told me what had happened while she made herself her bedtime tipple, which is camomile tea and a slug of Scotch.

'Melly went to a therapist this afternoon,' said Mum.

'Did she actually want to?' I said. 'Or did Janice make her?'

'It was Janice's idea,' said Mum. 'She still thinks what's happening is some kind of fixation the girls have got. But Melly thought it might help too, she says. The therapist – his name's Dr Wilson – had a cancellation this afternoon, but Janice couldn't make it. So she fixed for Melly to take the last hour off school, and Tina . . .' (this was another friend of Janice and Mum's) '. . . picked Melly up and drove her round, and she was going to wait at Dr Wilson's after the session until Janice collected her at half-past five. But soon after four Dr Wilson telephoned her at work and said she'd better come at once, so of course she did. When she got there she found Melly looking very shaky and dazed, and it was obvious that she'd been badly upset. Dr Wilson was seeing another patient by then, but he came out and said he thought it was all right to take Melly home, but she shouldn't be left alone and he'd telephone as soon as he could, and explain what had happened. Melly insisted she was all right, but she didn't want to talk . . .'

'Just like Melanie,' I said.

'Yes, I suppose so. Well, they got home and Melly seemed to settle down, and then Dr Wilson rang at about half-past six. Apparently Janice had told him what was going on, both about Melanie now, and about what had happened at Arles when she'd run away from the circus, so he'd asked Melly if she wanted to talk about any of that. She was quite open about it, he said, and was talking without any sense of strain or unease, though just like Melanie she tended to get upset at any suggestion that the two of them are actually two separate people, and then all of a sudden she regressed. Do you know what that means?'

'Went back?'

'Well, yes. They use it in some kinds of therapy. The therapist helps the patient go back to an earlier phase of life, sometimes almost as soon as they could walk or talk, and remember what it was like to be that child, and things that had happened to them then. It's more than just play-acting – it's as if they actually become that child . . .'

'Sounds interesting,' I said.

'I believe it can be,' she said. 'But it's not the sort of thing anyone should try without trained help. They probably wouldn't get anywhere, but if they did it might be really dangerous for them. Anyway, Dr Wilson wasn't even trying that with Melly when it happened. Without any warning she collapsed on to the floor and lay on her back with her arms and legs flailing and screamed and screamed like a very unhappy baby. Babies cry quite differently from small children, even. It's not a noise Melly could normally make, if she wanted to. Dr Wilson said he had never seen anyone regress so far back. And she wouldn't stop. He had great difficulty bringing her out of it. I think this must have been going on almost the same time that Melanie was having her outburst at the theatre.'

'It would be,' I said.

'When she did come back she was still extremely upset,' said Mum. 'She didn't want to talk about it, but later on she told Janice that she'd been blowing around in an empty grey place and there'd been a small door she couldn't get to . . .'

'You're going to tell Melanie about this, aren't you?'

'I expect so. Why?'

'Just tell her. Go on.'

'Well, Dr Wilson said that it looked as if something extremely traumatic had happened to Melly very early in life, and that possibly it was connected with being separated from her twin . . .'

'That doesn't work. It happened as soon as they were born.'

'But not as soon as they knew each other, darling. They'd been together for nine months before they were born.'

'You aren't serious, Mum?'

'I am, as a matter of fact, but don't let's argue about it now. I want to get to bed.'

'And I've got to finish my homework. Go on.'

'There isn't much more. Dr Wilson said, of course, that we'd all got to be extremely careful about how we approached that period of her life. The same applies to Melanie, I should think. We don't talk about it unless she positively wants to. And he also said that we should respect what the girls say about their meeting. If they believe it's dangerous, however much they long to meet, then they're probably right. We mustn't try to push them into a meeting until they themselves think they're ready.'

'He sounds as if he's got his head screwed on. I thought those types were all nutters.'

'Just what your father would have said, darling. Well, I'm going to bed . . .'

'One thing, Mum. You've got to make sure Janice does come this weekend. It's important. If Christine falls through again, I'll go down and be with Melly.'

'That's nice of you, darling. Let's hope it doesn't come to that.'

It didn't. Janice came, no fuss, and it worked out better than I'd expected. I'd been worried because Melanie had got used to plenty of hugs and cuddles from Mum, and Janice isn't like that. Her train didn't get in till after ten, and Mum took Melanie down to meet her at the station. When they arrived we had a hot drink and chatted for a bit in the kitchen, and then Mum and I went to bed to leave them alone. I was sleeping in the attic so Janice could have my room, so I didn't hear them come upstairs, but Mum said it wasn't till almost two in the morning.

Anyway the visit went all right. They weren't actually easy with each other at once, but you couldn't expect that. It must have been extremely weird for both of them. But they got on a lot better than I'd expected, because Janice is very prim and proper and has pretty old-fashioned ideas about a lot of things, and Melanie – she'd talked to me about this – had decided not to try and pretend that she wasn't what she was. I don't mean she swore and smoked the whole time, but she did a bit, and she was – well, Melanie, not Melly. The point is that Janice accepted it.

The other thing that happened was that Janice told us she'd found a private detective who could speak fluent French and she was going to ask him to go out to Arles and see if he could find anything out about what had happened fourteen years before.

'It isn't going to be cheap,' she said. 'But . . .'

'I'll go half,' said Mum.

'I wouldn't hear of it,' said Janice.

'Well, let's talk about it later,' said Mum. 'Go on.'

'There are two sides to it,' said Janice. 'The first is that we can't go on as we are, watching Melly and Melanie the whole time, worrying about them and so on. Something's going to give, and soon. We can all feel it. Besides, Melanie's my daughter. I want her to be able to come and live with me like a normal daughter. And I'm quite sure that the more we know – the less of this beastly mystery there is – the more chance we have of getting things right. I don't know how much this man will be able to find out, but he should at least be able to look up the birth records and so on. The French are very strict about records. I'm not insisting that Melly and Melanie are twin sisters, because they're both so determined that they aren't, but it's still the only explanation I can understand. That's one side. The other side is about me. Suppose I'd always thought Melly was my only daughter, and somebody told me that actually I'd had twins but one of them had died soon after she was born, it would still be very important to me to know if that was true. And since Melanie is here, and alive and well, and what's more since she's so obviously my daughter and no one else's, I really have got to know how it happened. I don't see how we can get things right between us until we know. That's what I mean about it being a beastly mystery. I don't like mysteries anyway, but this one's going to ruin our lives if we aren't careful. Isn't it, Melanie?'

'Too effing right it is,' said Melanie. 'Sorry, Ma. And we're never twins, but we've got to know, still.'

The detective's name was Eddie Droxeter. You'd never have known he was a detective to look at. 'Some kind of third-rate poet with indigestion,' Mum said. He had a long, pale face and a big mouth and sad eyes and he was tall and thin but he wore baggy clothes and stooped as if he was trying to make himself look shorter and less skinny. He was expensive, all right. Over a thousand pounds for a week, all in. Janice only had what she earned – she was a buyer for a small chain of clothes stores, so that was a lot for her. Mum told me she hadn't been able to persuade Janice to let her pay Melanie's share, and she hadn't pressed it too hard because she didn't want Janice to feel she was trying to take Melanie over, but she'd got her to accept an interest-free loan of half.

I liked Eddie. I may have made him sound a bit of an ass, but he was obviously pretty bright. He came up to Scotland to talk to Melanie about the circus, because she'd known it till only four years ago, and been part of it, while Janice had always been an outsider. To cut costs he came to Glasgow on one train and went back on the next, and I took Melanie down to meet him in the station tearoom, with other passengers hurrying in and out around us and the announcements booming away overhead.

He wanted everything she could remember, especially the name of anyone who might be persuaded to tell him something.

'There's none of them will talk to you,' Melanie said.

'Story of my life,' he said. 'Not being talked to. I'm expert at it. Seriously. This guy won't talk because he's an obstinate cuss, and this guy doesn't know anything, and this guy's scared, and this guy's got something to sell but wants to up the price, and this guy just wants another drink . . . All right, it's a circus, so there'll be acrobats. Let's make a list . . .'

It was interesting to watch how he really got Melanie going, and coaxed her on without wasting any time but without hurrying her either, getting her to talk about the people, not just the names but what kind of character they were, and remembering always that she'd been only ten when she'd left. I'd thought a thousand pounds plus was a lot of money for a week's work and he probably wasn't going to be worth it, but now I realized he might be.

At one point Melanie went off to the toilet and I asked him if he thought the girls were really twins, or something else.

'They've got to be,' he said. 'I go along with the theory that the father concealed the birth of one child, for some reason, and when the mother ran off with the one he regarded as *his* daughter he came and took her away and brought back the other one.'

'What about things like the scars on their arms?'

'That sort of thing happens with twins. I can't explain it. But for instance I was reading about twin brothers in America who'd been brought up separately, and when they finally met they were doing very similar jobs and wore almost identical clothes and their wives even had the same name as each other.'

'Weird.'

'There's a lot of weird stuff about twins. Now, before Melanie comes back, what can you tell me about the father? He's the obvious person for me to talk to, and barmen are used to strangers wanting to chat, but I'm leaving it till after Arles in case he smells a rat and alerts the people out there. He's not entirely sane on the subject of his daughter, right?'

'He's crazy,' I said, and started to tell him, but then Melanie came back and they went on with stuff about the circus until it was time for him to catch his train.

Eddie'd come up to see us the day before end of term. It was lucky it wasn't any earlier, because Melanie went through a bad patch while he was away, and not having to go to school meant I could be with her all day long. I don't mean that she was miserable, just incredibly wired and jumpy. Twanging from the moment she got out of bed till long after midnight, when Mum and I were dropping. She said her dreams were like that too, hurtling her along, strange and buzzing. She tried another of Mum's tranquillizers but it scared her.

'I came kind of loose,' she told me. 'I felt I was going to slip away out of myself, and wouldn't ever come back. I'd be in that empty place, other side of the wee door.'

Then sometimes she'd go into a kind of daze, for a couple of hours at a time. I took her out bird-watching with Ken once, and she had a great time making out she was a French hussy – Ken's so shy and proper he makes *me* look wild. He was interested in a pair of sparrow-hawks whose brood was almost ready to fly and he wanted to see it happen, and this meant lying still on a grassy ledge, where we could see the nest, for hours and hours. I didn't expect Melanie to stick it for more than ten minutes, but she barely stirred all afternoon. I nudged her when anything interesting happened at the nest, and she looked at it through Ken's binoculars in a dazed kind of way, but I wasn't sure she knew what she was seeing.

'Where've you been?' I asked her as soon as I could talk to her alone.

'Away,' she said. 'With Melly.'

'In Coventry?'

'Aye. No. She was here too. The place was nothing. I can't explain.'

'Was that . . . safe?'

'Aye. Like that. No problem.'

But mostly, like I said, she twanged, and it wore her out. When I'd first seen her she'd been exactly like Melly, and like Janice must have been when she was a kid, not fat, but a bit pudgy. Now she lost so much weight that you'd have said she was skinny, and her eyes were sunken and had that bruised look round them, but the eyes themselves glittered as if she was on speed or something, which she wasn't, of course.

I was worried for her, and I know Mum was too, so it was a great relief when Janice rang to say Eddie was back and he'd got news.

He came up to Bearsden to tell us himself what had happened. Now that I was home all day Mum had gone back to normal working hours, so we all got together in the evening.

The first thing Eddie had done was go to the *mairie* and look up the births register. He knew the exact day, so it wasn't difficult, and he found that one baby, Melanie Perrault, had been recorded. That didn't prove anything because Monsieur Perrault might have registered the other one under a different name and there were a couple of other girls born around then who might have been the other twin, but he did a bit more research and found that they were both real people and still alive.

Next he looked for the circus. It was on the road, so he hired a car and tracked it down in a little town up the Rhône valley. He went to a performance, and after it he asked to see the proprietor and said he was a TV researcher who was doing preliminary work for a programme about travelling circuses, and could he hang around with them for a day or two and talk to people? (Eddie had cards with the name of a bogus TV company on them – he said they were very useful sometimes.) He told the proprietor there'd be money coming if the programme was made, so of course he was interested. He was married to Melanie's Aunt Sylvie, by the way.

So Eddie did what he'd said, and hung around, and took photographs of everything, and asked questions, and stood people drinks, and so on. He was very careful about the questions he asked, to make them seem natural, but he pretended to be specially interested in the animals, and because there weren't any lions it was OK to ask if they'd ever had lions, and then why had the lion tamer left, and where was he now, because he might be interesting to talk to. Several people told him that Monsieur Perrault had suddenly sold his lions and cleared out, and they didn't know why, or where he'd gone.

'I was careful not to press it,' Eddie said. 'That first day all I was hoping to do was suss out which of them to try and go a bit further with. It wasn't going to be easy – I've come across professional criminals who were freer with information than that lot. But on the whole I thought I was getting along as well as I could hope, so I wasn't really ready next morning when this fellow turned up. I was having breakfast in my hotel and going through my notes when he came up to my table and pulled out a chair and sat down without so much as a by-your-leave.

'I said good morning, but he just sat and stared at me. I asked if there was something he wanted but he didn't say anything. I'd just about decided he was a nutter when he said, "There are these two girls, identical, now fourteen years old. They have learnt of each other's existence and now desire passionately to meet, but they are also afraid to do so. Correct?"

'He'd got me right off balance, but I managed to say something about it being an interesting story, and was there any more?

'"They do well to be afraid," he said. "They will have their desire very soon. You cannot prevent them. And when they meet they will die."

81

'He hammed it up by snapping his fingers when he said that, and that helped me get him placed. Melanie had described him to me, but I hadn't made the connection and I hadn't seen him at all around the circus. But I'd watched his performance. He was one of the clowns, and his act was to do bogus conjuring tricks which always went wrong – you remember Tommy Cooper? That sort of thing . . .'

'Monsieur Albert,' said Melanie.

'That's right,' said Eddie, 'but he called himself Albertus Magnus for his act, and at the critical moment he'd snap his fingers the way he'd just done. By now I'd got my wits about me enough to pretend I thought he was trying to interest me in a story for my TV company to produce, so I told him I'd need more, a lot more, before there'd be a hope of selling it to anyone. We beat around the bush quite a bit, and that allowed me to get a bit of a line on him. I put him down as a charlatan, but he obviously knew something, and he was prepared to sell it to me if the price was right. Tentatively I decided that he had probably helped in the original abduction . . .'

'No,' said Melanie. 'Papa couldn't abide him.'

'But Janice told me that he and your Aunt Sylvie were friends,' said Eddie.

'Not any more, they weren't,' said Melanie.

'That's very interesting,' said Eddie. 'Suppose he had helped with the abduction, he might then have tried to blackmail your father. That would account for a change of attitude. We still have to account for his knowing so much about you. Now, I think I was told that when you last saw your father you started to accuse him of what he had done to you when you were a baby. Did you actually tell him then that you knew about Melly's existence?'

'That I did,' said Melanie.

'Then he will almost certainly have guessed that you learnt about it from meeting Trish and Keith,' said Eddie. 'And also that they must know Janice, and would tell her, and that she would very likely want to know more. So he could well have written to his sister warning her that somebody might be making enquiries at the circus, in which case Monsieur Albert might also have learnt of it and decided to cash in on his knowledge. Most of what he said to me can be accounted for like that.'

'But not all of it,' said Mum. 'For instance, how would he have known about the girls wanting to meet and being afraid to? That isn't at all obvious. Anyone would expect that the very first thing we'd all want to do was arrange a meeting.'

'I don't pretend to account for everything,' said Eddie. 'I'm just saying that a lot of it can be rationally accounted for, so perhaps the rest can too. Shall I go on?

'I was still making out I thought he was trying to sell me a plot outline, and he was still ignoring that. After a while, to push the thing on a bit, I said that in any case my company wouldn't look at his story unless it had a happy ending, and was there any way in which the two girls could be brought together without some kind of tragedy?

'He sat and stared at me for a while, and then he said, "I can do it, and I alone. It must be done in a certain room in Arles, upon the nineteenth of August, at sunset. At no other time and in no other place can it be done, and by me alone. For me, personally, it will be both difficult and dangerous. My fee therefore will be a hundred thousand francs." That's about thirteen thousand pounds.

'Of course I said that there was no question of my company coming up with a sum like that on the basis of a sketchy verbal outline, but I went on pretending to negotiate in case he let something else slip. I didn't get very far, I'm afraid, because he saw what I was up to, and lost patience. He took a napkin and wrote an address on it and gave it to me and said, "Go back to England and talk to your friends. If they decide to make use of my services, come to this place at eight in the evening of the seventeenth of August. At this point I will explain to you what is required. All must be agreed by the evening of the eighteenth. Upon the nineteenth I will perform the operation. You will pay me ten thousand francs before I begin. Your friends will then have twenty-four hours in which to decide whether they are satisfied with the result. If they are you will then pay me the remaining ninety thousand. That is all I have to say." And he walked out.

'I tried again at the circus later that morning and they didn't want to know me. In fact they pretty well threw me out. And that's about it.'

Mum looked at Melanie and Melanie looked at the tablecloth.

Mum sighed. 'We've still got to go ahead,' she said.

'I was afraid you'd say that,' said Eddie.

Now I'm going to go back. I knew almost all of what Eddie had told us, because as soon as he'd come back from France he'd reported to Janice, and she'd phoned Mum and Mum had told me. Janice had been very upset about it and spent hours on the phone to Mum several evenings in a row.

'It seems quite mad,' Mum told me. 'In fact Eddie thinks we're being totally irresponsible, but we both believe this is something we've got to try. You've seen what Mclanie's been like these last few days. Melly's been the same. We all know they're working up to some kind of crisis. We can actually feel it coming . . .'

'On the nineteenth of August?' I said. 'Could be.'

'Janice left the circus on the eighteenth,' said Mum. 'So the nineteenth is fourteen years to the day since whatever it was happened to Melly when Monsieur Perrault took her away.'

'Monsieur Albert would know that, though,' I said. 'If he helped, I mean.'

'Yes, of course. But there are still some things he said to Eddie which I don't see how he could have known. Let me go on. You know what Janice is like. She's not the sort to go along with any kind of out-of-this-world explanation, but even so . . . You know what she said? "I feel as if Melly was dying of some kind of galloping cancer and there was this miracle cure which somebody told me about. If I was as desperate as I'm getting to be about this, I think I'd try it. It would be better than feeling guilty for the rest of my life because I hadn't."

'And there's something else. Dr Wilson has phoned a couple of times because he's worried about Melly, but Melly's absolutely adamant she doesn't want to see him again, and Janice daren't tell him any more than she has in case he decides he ought to get social workers in, and they'd almost certainly want to take Melanie into care, and perhaps Melly too. But at one point he said that it might be just as dangerous for the girls not to meet when they felt they were ready as it would be for them to meet when they weren't.'

'I'd go along with that,' I said. 'Melanie would go crazy. I mean crazy. Throw herself under a bus or something. I'm serious about that, Mum.'

'Janice has been saying almost the same thing about Melly,' said Mum.

The point about this was that Janice hadn't got thirteen thousand pounds, and she'd have needed quite a bit more, what with fares and hotels and so on, not to mention hiring Eddie again. And there was no way she could raise it. Mum could, because of my dad's insurance money. She'd bought our house outright, without a mortgage, but there was still a bit of a nest egg left. So a lot of the telephone calls to Janice were about persuading her to let

Mum use it. And the reason why Eddie had come to Bearsden was so that *he* could try to persuade her not to. She hadn't paid him to come. He'd done it on his own account because he was so unhappy about it.

'I think you're making a bad mistake,' he said.

'Tell me something,' said Mum. 'Don't you think ten thousand francs deposit is actually rather little for him to ask? I mean, if he's simply going to lay on some kind of conjuring trick so that he can walk off with our deposit, wouldn't he be asking more? Fifty thousand, I'd have thought. Doesn't that suggest he himself believes he can do what he says, so he's prepared to wait for the full fee?'

'All it suggests to me is that he thinks his conjuring trick is going to be good enough to persuade you he's done what he promised. That's why I'm not pulling out now, which I'm otherwise very inclined to. But I'm sticking with it because I believe you'll get into a worse mess without me than you will if I'm there.'

'Thank you,' said Mum.

We flew out to Marseilles on separate flights. Melanie didn't have a passport, but luckily Melly had one of her own as well as being still on Janice's, and of course the photograph was spot on, apart from the hair, so that was no problem. Eddie met us at the airport in a hired car and drove us to Arles across a flat, dusty, baking plain with dingy white cattle and vineyards. While he was driving us up he told us what had been happening. After that he was going back for Janice and Melly on the next flight.

'I'm not at all happy about this,' he said. 'In fact I'm still hoping I can get you to cry off. I'll refund my fee, if that will make the difference.'

'I wouldn't dream of asking you to do that,' said Mum, 'whatever else happens. You've been marvellous. But it's worse than we thought, is it?'

'You'll have to make your own minds up about that. I know what I think. I wish I could tell you this was some sort of straightforward scam, and he's just going to perform a lot of mystic passes and then pocket the fee. I could cope with that. But there's something else going on and I can't make out what. Anyway, I saw him yesterday evening. There didn't seem any point in going on with the story that I was some kind of film scout, so I told him I was acting on your behalf and you'd hired me to protect your interests. I then took up a fairly tough negotiating position – nothing he could object to if he was on the level, but plenty if he wasn't. The main point is that I've insisted on a legally enforceable contract, with all the money in the lawyer's hands until what he calls 'the operation' is completed to your satisfaction. I was expecting him to jib at that, but he didn't.

'Then I insisted on seeing the room where it was going to happen. It turned out to be in the building where I met him, which is an old inn out in the suburbs. He took me upstairs and showed me. It's a large room on the top floor. It looks as if some kind of club or something used to meet there once, but it's almost empty now. The point is that it can be reached by two sets of stairs at opposite ends of the building, so that the girls don't even have to use the same entrance before they finally meet. I went over it very thoroughly and I couldn't find anything wrong with it.

'Now I'll come to his demands. The first seems to me pure hocus-pocus but ought to be possible. The girls have to be identically dressed, and their hair identically cut and arranged. They have to be exact mirror images of each other. That means no fastenings on the dresses, and everything else symmetrical. If there's a pocket on the left breast there must be one on the right, and so on. I didn't get it about the fastenings until he showed me on my own shirt. My shirt buttons left over right, so my mirror image looks as if it buttons right over left . . .'

'I knew it was something to do with mirrors,' said Mum. 'You remember what happened in the Wardrobe, darling? And that's why their scars are on opposite arms. Go on, Eddie. There's bound to be a Carrefour or a Prisunic in Arles. I'm sure I can find some clothes for them there. And Janice will have to take Melly to a hairdresser and get her hair cut to match. Hell, we'll need a photograph.'

'That's OK,' said Eddie. 'I'll take one as soon as we get to the hotel. Now the next thing is a good deal trickier. Albert told me he'd be bringing an assistant. To push him a bit further I thought I might as well offer to do that myself, though I was

89

pretty sure he'd find some kind of occult nonsense reason to turn me down. Sure enough, he asked me when my birthday was, and when I told him May he said that wouldn't do because it had to be somebody born as near as possible to the cusp of Sagittarius and Capricorn, which I gather is just before Christmas – I'm not into astrology myself. Again I thought I might as well call him on that, so I told him I'd find somebody suitable, and very much to my surprise he accepted that at once. All he said was that it mustn't be a woman, and he gave me till this evening to come up with someone suitable. I spent an hour this morning ringing round the local agencies, but without any luck so far. It's not a big deal. We can always just tell him—'

'No,' said Mum. 'If we're going to go along with this at all we've got to do it properly. That means doing exactly what he says. Anyway, Keith's birthday is the twentieth of December. Is that any good?'

'Well,' said Eddie, 'I have to tell you I don't trust this guy an inch. He knows something, and he's up to something. No offence, Keith, but . . . Look, Trish, give me another hour, and if I don't come up with a genuine cusp-of-whatsit candidate I'll try Keith on him this evening. I'm seeing him in any case with the contract. And if I don't find someone and if he then turns Keith down, I'm going to do my damnedest to persuade you and Janice to call the whole thing off, after all.'

'We can't do that now,' said Mum. 'Not if we can possibly help it.'

'Let me tell you this,' said Eddie. 'I was trying to get him to agree what we meant by your being "satisfied with the operation" – you, Janice and both the girls, all of you happy, or what? Then I realized that he was talking as if there was only going to be *one* girl around when it was over.'

'That's right,' said Melanie.

She and I were in the back of the car and Mum was in front with Eddie. I'd been leaning forward to hear what Eddie was saying, but she'd spoken in such an odd way that I turned and looked at her. We'd all been having a very much easier time since Eddie had come back from France and it had been settled that we were going out to Arles. Melanie (and Melly too, Janice said) had stopped her wild fizzing and calmed down almost to normal. Beyond normal, even, because she'd spent most of the time in a sort of gentle daze, just waiting. 'Getting myself ready,' she told me. Now she was fizzing again all right. As I turned she grabbed me and whispered in my ear, 'Dinna let them back out now, Keith. Please! They canna do it now!'

'Do my best,' I whispered, and went back to listening to Mum and Eddie. Out of the corner of my eye I'd seen Eddie banging the side of his fist against the steering wheel, he was that upset.

'I don't get it!' he said. 'I absolutely don't get it! You're responsible adults. OK, you're a bit gone on the mumbo-jumbo yourself, but you're grown-up. And Janice doesn't believe a word of it. And yet you're both prepared to put these girls into the hands of this charlatan. Not to mention risking a considerable amount of money.'

'Is it really like that?' said Mum gently. 'I mean . . . No, look. We're upsetting Melanie. Get us to the hotel and take your photograph. And then – you've got a bit of time before you need to go back for Janice and Melly? – we'll talk about it then while Melanie and Keith are getting settled in. All right?'

Arles is roasting in August. There are shade trees down the main streets, but the heat bounces off the shabby plaster houses and the air crackles in your nostrils, and smells of dust and diesel fumes and garlic and cooking oil, and if there's a breeze you pick up wild, dry, herby smells from the baking plain. Your clothes stick to you and you stick to anything you sit on and you sleep under not even a sheet and you're still too hot.

Our hotel was in a quiet little back street and didn't look at all smart. (Janice and Melly were staying on the other side of the town.) Eddie took some pictures of Melanie with an instant camera, for the hairdresser, while we were still out on the pavement, and then Mum checked us in and Melanie and I waited upstairs while she talked with Eddie. We had tall, shuttered rooms with incredibly old-fashioned furniture. Mum and Melanie were in one room and I was in a sort of annexe off theirs.

Melanie was extremely jumpy until Mum showed up, just as bad as she'd been those first few weeks in Glasgow.

'I hope it's going to be all right,' Mum said. 'I think I've persuaded him to carry on for the moment anyway, though he still thinks we're taking a terrible risk with the girls. Which we are – there's no getting away from it – but anything else seems worse. And of course we've still got to see what Janice says.

'Eddie's going to see this Monsieur Albert this evening, and he's going to tell him straight out that we don't trust him, and that we've got to be absolutely sure that there's no way he can do any-thing to harm either of the girls. Eddie's got it into his head that he's going to try and make off with one of them by some sort of conjuring trick – he is a conjurer after all – so he's going to insist on there being someone from our side in the room the whole time – Keith if he can't find a grown-up who fits. If the man won't accept Keith then we'll know he's trying to cheat us, because Keith's perfectly gen-uinely on the cusp of Sagittarius and Capricorn. I've realized what that's about, by the way. We're almost on the cusp of Leo and Virgo at the moment, and the girls were born almost on the cusp of Aries and Taurus, and that makes a perfect triangle – I think it's called a trine, and it's supposed to be very significant, I don't remember why. So at least it wasn't something Monsieur Albert just made up as an excuse for not having Eddie.

'The other thing he's going to insist on is that we've got to be able to seal the room off completely, so that no one can get in or out from the moment it starts till it's over. Apparently there are two little rooms at the top of the two stairs – that's on either side of the big room, like lobbies. The doors lock, so we won't be able to interfere. Eddie's going to go over the whole place again this evening, and measure everything, and make sure there aren't any secret doors or compartments and so on. I must say I don't see how the man could possibly imagine he could get away with something like that. Surely the other girl . . . Anyway, if he turns us down over any of that, Eddie's going to call it off . . . I'm sorry, Melanie – I think we'll have to . . . God, I wish this was over. I'm absolutely sick with worry. I don't think I want any lunch.'

'I do,' I said.

'Me too,' said Melanie. 'I'm really hungry.'

It was strange. A few minutes before she'd been so jittery it almost hurt to watch, and now she'd calmed down completely. She'd barely seemed to register what Mum had been saying about calling things off if Monsieur Albert wouldn't agree, and now she lay on her bed and looked at the ceiling while Mum unpacked enough to change her shoes and so on.

'They must have landed by now,' said Mum as she got her things together for going out.

'A wee while back,' said Melanie. 'They're in the terminal now, showing their passport. There's a bairn behind them, crying.'

'If you could do that on the stage you'd make a fortune,' said Mum, but she sounded cross about it.

We went out and found a store and bought long French loaves and butter and cheese and peaches and Coke, and made ourselves a picnic in the shade of some trees in a hot little square with a dribbling fountain in the middle. Then we went off to find the clothes, with Melanie drifting along in a kind of happy daze, letting herself be pushed and shunted round this enormous superstore while we looked for absolutely mirror-image dresses. Everything seemed to have a little logo on one side, or a pocket, or something. At last we found two bright yellow shift things with zips at the back. Melanie just glanced at them and said, 'Yuck,' but Mum and I went over them inch by inch looking for some way of telling them apart.

'I suppose they'll do,' said Mum. 'Only I wish they weren't so hideous.'

We were trying on sandals, and Melanie had hold of my shoulder while she balanced on one leg getting her heel right in the other foot, when she froze. Her nails dug into me like claws.

'Ouch!' I said. 'You needn't do that!'

She didn't hear me. She stuck there, except that her head turned slowly as if she was watching something extraordinary going along the next aisle. Then she relaxed.

'What was that about?' I said.

'They were driving by,' she whispered. 'In the road just out there.'

From then on, for the rest of the day, she was a quite different sort of dreamy – quiet, smiling, doing little dance steps while she walked, breaking off in the middle of something she was saying for a few seconds and then carrying on, as if she'd just said hello to a friend who'd passed by. Mum paid for the things she'd bought and went off to talk to Janice and Eddie while Melanie and I walked slowly back to the hotel along the shady side of the streets, turning off to look at anything that seemed interesting. Melanie too. Being interested, I mean – even more than me. It was as if she kept saying, 'Look! Look!' to somebody I couldn't see was there.

We stopped at a café and had what was their idea of tea – in a glass, just hot water, with your own teabag which you put into it, and no milk, but French milk is disgusting anyway. Then we got a bit lost, so we weren't back at the hotel until only just before Mum. I'd been expecting problems, in fact I thought Eddie might have persuaded Janice to call the whole thing off. I mean she saw things almost the same way as he did. But no.

Mum told me about it while Melanie was in the shower.

'She'd already told him she thought we had to go ahead,' she said. 'Before I got there, I mean. She says Melly might crack up completely if we don't. She's worried, of course, but she's a bit more down-to-earth about it than I am. She says the only thing that matters is that the girls are convinced this is the right way for them to meet, and it makes no difference if Monsieur Albert's a complete charlatan. In fact what would be worrying would be if he wasn't. She says he can't really expect us to believe there'll only be one of the girls left at the end of it, that's just mumbo-jumbo, and of course they'll both be there and he'll claim he was talking metaphysically, or something, but it's worth letting him see he's not going to get away with trying anything like that. And tomorrow morning she's going to look for some sort of paging gadget for you to have on you, so that you can call us the moment you think there's anything wrong.'

'All right,' I said.

'You're sure, darling? You'd say, wouldn't you?'

'Yes, of course,' I said.

Actually I didn't know what I felt. All this was making me pretty anxious. I couldn't think properly. One side of me agreed with Eddie and Janice, that Monsieur Albert was a crook, a conman, and all he was probably after was Mum's money, though he might try something nasty with the girls and it was up to me to stop it. That's what my brain said. But another side of me – well, I'd spent so much time with Melanie, and I minded so much for her and about her, and she was so sure that this thing mattered more than anything else in the world . . . well, I believed that too. I had to.

Not just that. I was actually praying that Eddie didn't find someone else with the right birthday. I was scared stiff, but I wanted to be there. Me and no one else.

We waited for it to get a bit cooler, but it didn't, so in the end we went out and had supper at a restaurant in one of the main squares, with tables out on the pavement. Just being with Melanie now was like being on some kind of wonderful high, she was so happy, bubbling and chatting, and then going dreamy for a few minutes, and then coming back to us and telling us what Melly and Janice were up to. I could almost feel them, Melly and Melanie, swooping to and fro between their two bodies like the swifts swooping and wheeling against the evening sky.

'I don't know if I can bear this much more,' Mum whispered to me at one point. 'It'll be so agonizing if it all goes wrong.'

'Not much longer now,' I told her.

But it was. It was for ever. The night was for ever, and the morning longer, and the afternoon longer still, and I'd look at my watch thinking that would be another twenty minutes gone and it was maybe three. The heat made it worse. It was almost as if time had sort of melted, like a road melts on really hot days, and everything stuck to it as it went along.

Eddie came round soon after breakfast. He talked to Mum alone for a bit. Melanie seemed to have gone all sleepy. She said she didn't want to talk or think because she was getting herself ready. She seemed perfectly happy, but we didn't want to leave her alone, so I waited with her until Mum came up and told me that Eddie hadn't found anyone else and he needed to tell me what I'd got to do.

I went down feeling nervous as hell and we sat in a dark, hot little bar smelling of last night's smoke and drink while he explained.

'I saw him again yesterday evening,' he said, 'and I got most of what we wanted. I wasn't expecting the lot. The chief thing I didn't get was that he wouldn't hear of anyone waiting in the two lobbies at the top of the stairs. The whole of that floor has to be free of irrelevant astral influences, believe it or not. At least the bastard's consistent. But we can wait on the landings below, and we can see the top of the stairs from there, and that's pretty well as good. I've got a French colleague coming from Marseilles to give a hand, so that means there will be two each side. And I've been over the whole place again, measuring up, and I'd bet my life there's no other way out.'

'He didn't mind?' I said.

'Didn't turn a hair. Amused, if anything, but he doesn't give much away. The other thing he wouldn't stand for was me taking you round there this morning to show you the layout. More astral contamination, of course. Best I can do is a sketch map. I made him take me through the whole process, as far as it concerns you. This wasn't just so that I could check it out. It's so that if he tells you anything different you'll know he's up to something. And he is. I'm still dead certain of that.'

He unfolded a piece of paper and showed me his sketch. It was not quite square, with two smaller squares in the corners on one of the long sides, leaving a space like a fat T. This was the main room. The small squares were the two lobbies, with stairs leading up to them.

'Right,' he said. 'There are four good windows, so there should be plenty of light. Once the proceedings have begun, Albert will be at this end here, and you will be where I've marked, behind the mirror. I haven't seen the mirror, but he says it's a bit under a metre wide and about twice that high. He wanted to put you right down here by the back window, but I insisted that you must be able to see him throughout the proceedings. He didn't like it, but in the end he agreed on condition that once things are under way you keep absolutely still and don't do anything to distract him. By the way, I haven't told him that you'll have a pager, assuming Janice can find one.

'When you first come into the room, take a good look round. Apart from the mirror there'll be only what's already there – that's to say this stack of chairs in the corner and this table here. The table-cloth hangs down a few centimetres. If he's moved it or changed it so that it prevents you from seeing under it except by lifting it up, object. That's the only hiding place I can see in the room, and I think it's too obvious for him to consider. There are little balconies outside the three main windows. Take a look out and check there's no one on them.

'When you're satisfied, tell him, and he'll then go through the procedure with you. I've told him that you understand simple French, provided he speaks

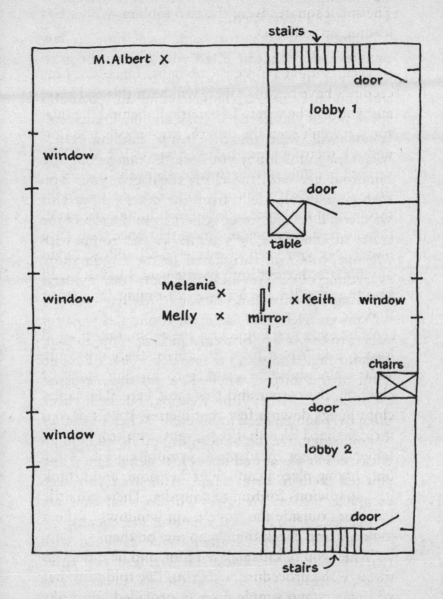

The upstairs room at the Orangerie

slowly and clearly. All right? Now this is what he says is going to happen.

'Sunset is at eight forty-six, local time. A few minutes before that he'll tell you to fetch the girls. You come to this lobby here, go to the top of the stairs and beckon to Melanie to come up. You don't speak unless you have to. Trish and my French colleague will wait on the lower landing. Once Melanie's in the lobby you lock the outer door and blindfold her with the cloth she'll give you. You then go and call Melly from the other lobby. This way, you'll be able to see Albert from the top of the stairs all the time he's alone in the room with Melanie, and you can signal to me if you think everything's OK. You lock that door – don't worry, I'll bring a jemmy – and blindfold Melly.

'You go back into the main room and wait for Albert to tell you to bring the girls in. You do that, Melanie first, and stand them back to back here, in front of the mirror, where I've put these crosses. He's seen what they'll be wearing, but he'll check them over and go back to his chair. When he signals to you to remove the blindfolds you do so, and go back behind the dotted line. He'll signal again, and you tell them to turn round. After that you keep complete silence. The girls will do what they are compelled to do, he says, whatever that means.

'The mirror has a leather cover, fastened with two buckles at the back. He'll ring a bell three times, twice for you to undo the two buckles, and the third time for you to remove the cover. You fold

102

it and put it on the table and you then move to your spot behind the mirror and stay there, until . . .'

'Will I be able to see the girls from there?' I said.

'No, you won't. I couldn't shake him on that. This was the best I could get. He says it's not to stop you seeing the girls, but so that they aren't distracted by seeing you. They mustn't be aware of anything except the mirror. But you'll be able to see him and everything else except that narrow section of the room, and I don't see what he can get up to from where he is. That window is three storeys up a sheer wall with a busy square outside. That curtain will be closed, by the way, but he's leaving the other two open for light.

'All right? Then you stay in your chair until everything's over. He'll ring the bell again for you to put the cover back on the mirror and fasten the buckles. You don't need to wait for him to ring three times. And that's apparently it. You can unlock the doors and we'll come up and check that the girls are all right.'

'Did he actually say girls? Two of them?' I said.

'No, he didn't. He's still going through this charade of pretending there's only going to be one of them. Right up to the point when you take the cover off he was talking about '*les jeunes filles*', and from then on it's '*la jeune fille*'. I know it's nonsense, and I'm dead certain there's nothing he can do to make it happen, but it makes me bloody uneasy and I wish to hell I'd never got into this.'

*

103

After Eddie had gone we got through the day somehow. I just remember the heat, and the sweating
tourists, and a café with air-conditioning where we
had ice creams, and the way the sun slammed into
us when we went outside again, and the stuck
minutes. I don't think Melanie noticed anything at
all. She was in a different kind of dream today, not
soaring about, but sleepwalking round with us.

She actually managed to sleep after lunch. I just
lay on my bed and sweated, and Mum read. By
teatime I was too nervous to stay there any more, so
I decided to go out again, though it wasn't any
cooler. Melanie woke up and said she was coming
too, so we went back to the café and had Cokes. She
seemed wide awake now, but very quiet and
solemn, so I didn't try to chat. Time oozed by.

We were on our way back to the hotel when
Melanie took my hand and said, 'I've a thing to tell
you, Keith. It came to me while I was asleep. But
first you must promise me you won't say a word of
it to Trish or Janice or Eddie.'

Once, after some mess I'd got myself into at
school, Dad had told me what to do if somebody
asks you this. You say, 'If it's something I *can*
promise.' But you don't, of course – certainly not if
it's someone like Melanie who asks you.

'All right,' I said.

'I ken now why Papa sold his lions,' she said. 'He
didn't want this day to come. He couldn't just leave
and go to another circus, because Monsieur Albert
would find him there, easy. But he thought maybe if

104

he crossed the sea . . . Edinburgh would be a good long way . . . But it was never enough . . . Papa loved his lions more than anything in the world. But he sold them for me.'

'I suppose that means he loved you more than the lions,' I said.

She looked at me sideways and smiled. I knew why, because I'd heard the silly jealousy in my own voice.

'Why don't you want me to tell Mum and the others?' I said, to cover up.

'Because Eddie's right. You can't trust Monsieur Albert. He'll be trying something.'

'But what? I mean, if he does what we want without any cheating at all he's going to get a lot of money.'

'I dinna ken. But he'll be trying something yet.'

When we got back to the hotel we found that Eddie had been and left a sort of electronic gadget for me which Janice had found. I'm going to go on calling it the pager, though I don't know what it was really for. It looked like a pencil torch. There were two of them and Eddie was keeping the other one. They each had a button on them which you could press, and when you did the light on the other one lit up and it gave a buzz. Mum and Eddie had tested it, and it worked from the street outside up to our rooms in the hotel. I dug out a shirt with a breast pocket and put it in there with a couple of pens. It looked like the sort of thing a kid carries around anyway.

Then we had a bit over half an hour left before our taxi came. I felt extremely nervous again. Time went slower than ever and I kept swallowing and feeling sticky-chilly in spite of the heat, and getting up and walking around and sitting down again, and not being able to concentrate on anything for more than a couple of minutes. Mum read, and Melanie, in her yellow dress, lay on her bed with her eyes shut, but she wasn't asleep.

When the taxi came it took us a fair distance, right out of the touristy parts, past a lot of ugly modern flats, to a bit where the buildings were old again. I guessed this must have been a village right outside Arles, once, and then Arles had grown round it. We stopped in a grubby square with a church on one side and trees in the middle, where men were playing that game which is a bit like bowls, except that the balls are made of steel and you throw them through the air. The houses had heavy dark shutters and brown or orange plaster, peeling and soft-looking. The roadway was cobbles. Noisy little vans buzzed and bumped across them.

Round from the church the pavement was broad enough to hold a few tables, where men were playing dominoes and drinking beer or wine. The tables belonged to the hotel. It looked so shabby you couldn't imagine anyone wanting to stay there. Its name, L'Orangerie, was written in dark green paint across its front.

The men at the tables gave Mum the eye as she

led the way in. Melanie drifted along in a kind of trance. I had to hold her elbow and steer her.

Eddie was waiting for us in the lobby. He led us along a corridor and up two flights of stairs to a landing where he introduced us to the detective from Marseilles, who'd come to help. His name was Pierre.

'All set?' said Eddie. 'We've still got about twenty minutes till kick-off, but Keith should go up straight away and meet our friend. Just give me a minute to get round to the other side, Keith, then carry on up these stairs and through the door at the top. You'll find yourself in a small room with another door on the far side. Knock, and wait till he tells you to come in. After that, carry on as we've arranged, and if he tells you anything different, you do what I said. Don't argue with him. Just do it. And if there are any problems, send for me. OK? Well, good luck. See you later.'

We counted sixty seconds on my watch, and then Mum kissed me and wished me luck. Melanie just smiled vaguely at me. I wasn't sure she even knew I was there.

I climbed the stairs with my heart hammering, opened the door at the top and went through into a little square dusty room with one small window and not a scrap of furniture. I knocked on the door on the far side, waited until a voice said, '*Entrez,*' and went in.

For a moment I could hardly see. The room faced west, and the setting sun was blazing in through three tall windows which ran right down to the floor. The light from the middle one was straight in my eyes, dazzling after the darkness of the stairs, but hazy too, and the air was full of a horrible sweet, oily smell. I bumped into a table and felt my way round out of the direct sun, where I could see.

The right-hand window was open and a man was standing there, looking out over the trees in the square and the jumbled roofs to watch the sun go down. He was smoking a funny short pipe with a tiny bowl. That was where the haze was coming from. It wasn't pot – I know what that smells like.

It was incredibly hot up there, in spite of the open window. It was right up under the roof and the sun had been beating down on the tiles all day. I thought I'd been sweating like a pig already, but now it really streamed off me. And the air was foul to breathe, too, with that sweet, sticky smoke mixed in with the dry, hot dust.

The man didn't move, so I took a look round. The room seemed pretty much like Eddie had told me, with the stack of chairs down at the bottom beside the far window, and the table in the corner where he'd drawn it. I took a special look at the tablecloth, which was a grubby old red thing with tassels at the corners. It hung only a little way down and I decided it must be the same one he'd seen.

Eddie hadn't seen the mirror, but that was where he'd drawn it too, opposite the middle window. It was about as tall as I am, but all I could see of the mirror itself was a round stand of very dark wood, right at the bottom. The rest of it was covered by a sort of black leather sheath, very old and crackled, with two straps that buckled behind.

I opened the middle window and looked out. There was a tiny balcony – really it wasn't much more than a railing to stop people falling out – but there wasn't anyone hiding out there or on either of the other two, so I came back in and waited there, thankful for the outside air.

At last the man turned round and beckoned, and I went over. He looked at me for a while, so I looked back. He was short and square with big, trembling hands. He was half bald, and the rest of his hair was clipped short. His eyes seemed extra large, and soft, and deep. His face was brown but had a funny dead look to it, like your hands go when you've kept them a long time under water. (I'd seen a programme about retired clowns once, and one of them had skin like that. He said it was from the old-style make-up.)

After a bit he said, 'Bon. *Eh bien, tu t'appelles* Keet?'

His voice was quiet and flat, and came a lot through his nose. He sounded tired and bored.

'*Oui*, Keith,' I said.

He nodded and took me through my instructions in French, in the same order as Eddie had done. I was shuddering with nerves inside, and I thought the easiest thing was to act a bit dumb. We looked into the two little rooms I was going to bring the girls through. The other one was no different from the one I'd already seen. He showed me where he wanted me to make the girls stand, and the signals he'd give me to take the blindfolds off and then to tell them to turn round. Then he took me behind the mirror and unfastened and refastened the top buckle, and made me do the same. He told me to wait and fetched a small handbell out of his bag. I think it may have been silver, but it was almost black.

'*Je sonne une fois,*' he said, and shook the bell, holding the clapper with his other hand so that it didn't actually ring. '*Tu défais la première boucle.*'

He mimed undoing the top buckle, and looked at me. I nodded. He shook the bell again.

'*Au deuxième coup, la deuxième boucle,*' he said, and mimed undoing the other strap. This time he waited a bit before he shook the bell.

'*Au troisième coup, tu ouvres l'enveloppe et tu l'enlèves.*'

He put the bell on the table, still making sure it didn't ring, and mimed sliding the cover off round the mirror from behind.

'*Exactement comme ça,*' he said, and made me stand where he'd stood and do what he'd done.

With his finger he drew an imaginary line from the corner of the table across the room behind the mirror.

'*Tu ne dépasses jamais cette ligne,*' he said, speaking even slower than he had been doing. '*Et tu ne regardes jamais dans le miroir. Jamais, jamais, jamais.*'

110

'Right,' I said, miming it all again as I went through it. 'The first time you ring the bell I undo the top strap. The second time I undo the bottom strap. The third time I take the cover off. I mustn't cross this line and I absolutely mustn't ever look in the mirror.'

'*Bon*,' he said, and went and fetched a chair from the stack and put it behind the mirror.

'*Alors*,' he said, '*tu plies l'enveloppe et le mets sur la table, et tu t'assieds ici. Puis tu ne bouges plus jusqu'à la fin.*'

I went and sat in the chair to check how much I could see. I wasn't slap up against the mirror, so the only bits of the room which were hidden were a wedge of space in front of the mirror and two narrow triangles round the corners on either side of me. But the chair where Monsieur Albert would be sitting was well in sight, and so were both the end windows, while I could just see the top of the middle one above the mirror. The windows themselves were double and opened inwards, so even when the curtains were closed I didn't see how anyone could come in that way without moving them enough for me to notice.

'I get it,' I said. 'I fold the cover and put it on the table, and then I come and sit in this chair and don't move till it's all over.'

'*Bon*,' he said, and went back to his window and his pipe. I got up and checked the back windows, including the two in the lobbies, but they didn't seem to open at all, so I went to the chair and sat there looking round and trying to think if there was anything else I could do.

The sun was almost down and streaming flat across the room when Monsieur Albert knocked out his pipe on the window frame and came and closed the centre window and drew the curtains, darkening all that part of the room but leaving the two shafts of light streaming in at either end, golden in the dusty, smoky air. I was all tensed up, peering for the slightest sign that he was trying to trick us, and I knew that something had bothered me, some other movement I'd seen out of the corner of my eye as he'd closed the curtains. Then I spotted what it must have been. He'd left the window nearest him open, and the far half of it was at an angle to the room with its dark curtain hanging behind it, so what I'd seen was the reflection of the central shaft of sunlight being blanked out. It wasn't important . . .

Yes it was – it might be! What I could mainly see was the reflection of the blaze of light across the other end of the room, striking the two walls of the lobby as far as the door on my left, but right at the edge of it was the beginnings of a dark shape which I realized was the very edge of the mirror. There was nothing else it could be. The reflection was a bit wavy because the glass was old, but the bit of the mirror was surprisingly clear against the brightness beyond. Please, please don't let him shut the window, I thought as he went back that way, and he didn't. He settled into his chair, opened his bag, checked through the stuff inside and looked up.

'*On commence*,' he said. '*Fais entrer les deux filles. Uniquement les deux filles.*'

I went through the lobby on my right, opened the far door and beckoned to Melanie. Mum kissed her and she climbed slowly up the stairs, looking calm and serious. I held the door for her and locked it behind us. She waited in the middle of the room and gave me a red scarf which I folded into a loose roll and tied over her eyes.

'Good luck,' I whispered, and she smiled, but as if she wasn't sure what I was talking about.

When I crossed the room on my way to the other lobby Monsieur Albert was sitting with his hands folded and his head bowed, as if he was praying. I went to the top of the stairs and beckoned to Melly and gave the thumbs-up to Eddie, to tell him that so far it had all gone as he'd fixed. But when Melly came climbing towards me I stood and gaped and almost forgot everything, because she wasn't Melly, she was Melanie. The room and the stairs were the other way round, and it was a green scarf she gave me, not a red one, and I knew with my mind that this was Melly because it had to be, but I still couldn't make myself believe it, especially when she smiled exactly the same smile when I wished her luck. I thought I'd known how like they were, but now that they'd got their hair the same I realized I hadn't, the likeness was so amazingly exact. I don't think even Janice could have told them apart. I'd finished tying the blindfold before I remembered to check back through the door and see what

Monsieur Albert was up to, but he was still where I'd left him, huddled on his chair with the bald top of his head glistening with sweat. He looked up when he heard the door close and put his finger to his lips. I nodded to tell him everything was ready.

He pointed to the other lobby, so I went and fetched Melanie, leading her by the hand to the exact place he'd shown me. Then Melly. When they were back-to-back in front of the mirror he got up and went into each of the lobbies in turn and tried the outside doors to make sure I'd locked them. Then he came back and looked very carefully at the two girls, starting at their sandals and working up. He adjusted the shoulder of Melly's dress, and then spent some time comparing their hair. After a bit he took a small pair of scissors out of his pocket and snipped a wisp of hair off the back of Melanie's head and another by Melly's left ear. He was careful not to drop the stuff he'd cut, but took a brown envelope out of his pocket and popped it in. He was putting the envelope back when he seemed to change his mind and handed it to me. I put it in the back pocket of my jeans.

He pointed to tell me to go back behind the imaginary line on the floor, so I did that, checking over my shoulder that he was going back to his chair. He sat down and started to fish things out of his bag, first a piece of cloth which might once have been white but now was a sort of brownish-cream with darker stains on it. He spread it carefully on the floor in front of him and then one at a time took several little packages out of the bag, unwrapped them and arranged what was in them on the cloth. One was a small brass cup, which he placed upside down. Another looked like a chicken's foot, but very old and dried. There was a dark blue stone and a lump of something wrapped in a yellow bandage, like a mummy. I couldn't see what the other things were. I think there were seven of them. He put them in a circle and drew with his finger in the air between them, in the shape of a star, finishing where he'd begun, over the cup. He took some powder out of a small tin box, shaking it into the palm of his hand, and dribbled it into the centre of the circle in a thin stream, moving his hand so that it made some kind of pattern on the cloth. He sat staring at it for a while before he looked up and gave me the signal to remove the blindfolds.

I did that and went back to my place.

He raised his hand and made a circle with his finger in the air.

'You can turn round now,' I croaked.

They turned, opposite ways, moving exactly together as if they'd rehearsed and rehearsed it. They looked at each other just as if each of them was seeing herself in a mirror, and they each put up the same hand to fiddle with the same bit of hair, the way girls do when they spot themselves in a window or something. They smiled and put up both hands and touched, palm to palm. Their happiness was beautiful. It filled the room. I forgot my nerves and the stink of smoke and the awful dusty heat and just stared. Now at last I understood what Melanie had been telling me all along – she and Melly weren't two girls who happened to look amazingly like each other, they were one girl, only there happened to be two of her.

I didn't come to until I heard the bell ring. That reminded me that I'd got Monsieur Albert to keep an eye on as well, so as soon as I'd got the top buckle undone I looked to see what he was up to. He was crouched forward over the cloth, concentrating on it as if it was the only thing in the world, streaming with sweat and muttering under his breath.

When I looked back to the girls they had taken hold of each other's hands and were circling slowly round, face to face. I didn't know how many turns they'd done so now I really couldn't say which was which. They were still smiling, but now it wasn't just simply and peacefully, like somebody waking from a good dream, but – I don't know – as if they were sharing a secret they knew, and no one else did.

Out of the corner of my eye I saw Monsieur Albert ring the bell again, reaching out and picking it up and shaking it without stopping his muttering or looking away from the stuff on the cloth. I undid the second buckle and waited with my hands on the top of the cover ready to slide it round and off. It seemed to be quivering slightly under my touch, but that was probably only my nerves.

The girls were circling faster now, swinging each

other round with their feet almost touching and their bodies leaning apart and their heads thrown back, laughing aloud too and circling faster and faster so that if either of them had made a mistake they'd have fallen in a heap, but they went on speeding up till they seemed to be moving faster than they could have possibly swung on their own, as if something had hold of them and was spinning them like a top till their shifts were a yellow dizzying blur . . .

The bell rang, long and loud. The cover was heavier than I'd expected and I thought for a moment that I was going to knock the mirror crooked, but it stuck where it was as if it was bolted to the floor. I laid the cover on the table and began to fold it by feel, looking over my shoulder to watch the girls. They were slowing down, slowing down. They ought to have been too dizzy to stand, and they did look dazed, lost, but they were held. I could actually see that. Something was holding them, controlling them. I remembered what Monsieur Albert had said to Eddie, that they'd 'do what they were compelled to do'.

I didn't like it. It scared me. Up to now I'd been nervous about the girls meeting because we'd built it up into such a big thing, and I'd been doubly nervous about it being up to me to spot whatever kind of trickery Monsieur Albert might get up to. But those were ordinary sorts of nerves. Now for the first time I really felt – I *knew* – that something was happening which there wasn't any kind of ordinary explanation for. Besides that, it meant that Monsieur Albert had actually known what he'd been talking about, and I'd better do exactly what he'd told me, or everything might go wrong.

I looked down and saw that I'd managed to fold the cover into a neat roll – it could almost have folded itself, because I hadn't been noticing what my hands were up to. I'd even fastened it with one of its buckles. I went back to my chair and sat down, hitching it forward a couple of inches as I did so – the way you do, but I did it on purpose, because it meant I could see a scrap more of the mirror in the reflection from the window pane. I couldn't see the actual girls at all from where I sat, but they were right in the middle of the reflection, a bit wavy and hard to make out, but there all right. They were turning very slowly now, close together, with their hands under each other's elbows and their bodies almost touching.

As I watched, the light in the room changed. It seemed to happen almost in an instant, as the sun went down and the golden shafts of sunlight at either end of the room went dim. I glanced at Monsieur Albert. I didn't want him to catch me staring at the reflection in the window, but he wasn't. He seemed to be in a sort of trance, stiff but quivering, with his hands held tense in front of his shoulders, cupped, palms forward, fingers spread, while he gazed unblinking at the girls. He wasn't seeing me at all, so I looked back at the window reflection.

I could see the girls better now. Before, I'd been looking through one shaft of dusty sunlight and they'd had the other one behind them, so they'd just been a couple of dark outlines. Now I could just about see their faces, both in profile because they'd stopped turning and were standing one with her back to the mirror and the other facing her. They looked solemn but not sad, like dancers in a dream.

Moving exactly together they raised their hands and touched palms, the way they'd started their dance. Slowly they moved towards the mirror until the nearest one had her back right against it.

They didn't stop there. She went on, into the mirror. I'd only seen it with the cover on it, and even then it wasn't more than a couple of inches thick, but she slid right into it, slowly, her arms and hands going last of all. I could just see her left hand in the bit of mirror at the edge of the reflection, with the other girl's right hand resting on the glass. They stayed there and didn't move.

Monsieur Albert gave a sort of shuddering sigh, which reminded me again that I was supposed to be watching him too. He was leaning back in his chair with his eyes closed and gasping like a runner after a race. The sweat was dripping off the tip of his nose, his face glistened and his shirt looked as if someone had turned a hose on him.

I looked at the reflection in the pane, and saw that the girl who was still in the room was backing slowly away from the mirror, still in her open-eyed dream. She stopped, and I watched her beginning to wake up. Her hand went up to her hair and fiddled with it, just like at the beginning. She smiled. She was happy. It had worked. It was all right.

She stayed like that, gazing at the mirror. I guessed she had to, that she couldn't look away until it was covered up, so I turned to Monsieur Albert, waiting for him to ring his bell, but he was busy with his things on the cloth again. He took the cup and put it, right-way up this time, in the middle, and moved the other objects closer in around it. He took an envelope out of his pocket, shook something from it into his palm, and carefully poured whatever it was into the cup. He tucked the envelope into the bag. Then he took a small stone bottle out of the bag, uncorked it and dripped two or three drops of liquid on to the other stuff in the cup.

He held his hands out over the cloth as if he was warming them at a fire, and concentrated. I could feel the effort of his concentration. I think a little smoke came out of the cup – I'm not sure . . .

And then I saw him relax. He straightened, and looked up, and smiled.

I don't know how to describe it, but it was obvious. He was watching something really nasty happen, and he was loving it.

I looked at the window pane to see what he was seeing.

The whole of the middle of the room seemed much darker now – I'm not sure about that either, and anyway night comes quickly that far south. The girl was still there, in front of the mirror, just her shape against the light from the other window. She had her arm thrown up in front of her face as if she was fighting not to go on looking in the mirror but she couldn't help it. She was held, compelled . . .

I don't mean I could see anything holding her, but I could see *how* it was holding her, how it was stopping her getting her arm over her eyes, making her look, and then beginning to force her in towards the mirror, though she was leaning away from it, with her other arm up now, pushing at nothing, fighting not to get any nearer, but all the time being forced slowly in . . .

I didn't think. I just knew it was wrong. There wasn't any time for the cover. I jumped up and tried to knock the mirror over but it was like hitting a house. Monsieur Albert was screaming at me. I grabbed the tablecloth with both hands and swung it over the mirror. It floated out as if there'd been a wind underneath it, but I tugged it down my side and rushed round and took the girl by the arm and yanked at her.

For a moment she didn't budge, but then a flapping end of the cloth got in front of her face and she came with a rush and we both went sprawling back behind the mirror. As I fell I saw the girl's hand going out and grabbing the tablecloth to stop herself from falling, and pulling it clear just as Monsieur Albert came rushing across . . .

He stopped. No he didn't. He *was* stopped. Dead. I was on my back and beginning to scramble up and I saw it happen. One moment he was going

121

full tilt and the next he was stuck. He ought to have fallen flat on his face but he didn't, because he was held. Compelled.

Slowly he turned to face the mirror. He stared at it. His face was grey under the tan. He took a deep breath, squared his shoulders, gave a little nod and walked steadily into the mirror. It didn't take long. I don't know – ten seconds . . .

Then, far too late, I remembered the pager and fished it out and pressed the button. I finished scrambling up and knelt by the girl. She was lying on her front with her head turned sideways and her eyes closed. I could hear Eddie starting to break his way in through the door, but I couldn't leave her alone to go and unlock it. I felt I had to get her as far away from the mirror as possible, so I rolled her over and took her under the arms and dragged her down to the bottom of the room. I'd just got her there when Eddie and Mum came bursting in.

Eddie took a quick look round and ran to the other room. I heard him unlocking the door. Mum rushed down to where we were.

'Where've they gone?' she said. 'Where's . . . Oh, God, what's happened to her? Which is this one?'

I just stood, shaking my head. I was shuddering, and sopping with sweat, and my head was pounding. I had a horrible sick feeling that I'd ruined everything, barging in like I had. Janice was there now, kneeling by the girl and sobbing, 'Melly! Melly, darling! Is it you . . . ?' And Eddie and the other man, Pierre, were talking, arguing behind us.

The girl's eyes half opened. We all hushed.

'I'm here. It's me,' she whispered. Melly's voice.

'Where's Melanie then?' said Mum.

Dreamily the girl smiled.

'I'm here. It's me – together, I'm telling you.' Melanie's voice.

There was a noise on the stairs, somebody running up, several people. Quickly Eddie and Pierre moved out into the lobby to meet them. Men's voices then, loud, arguing in French, too fast for me. Eddie came to the door and beckoned to me, so I went over.

There were three of them. I think I'd noticed them at one of the tables outside the hotel when we'd arrived. They looked pretty tough and determined.

'These appear to be friends of Monsieur Albert's,' said Eddie. 'They want to know what happened to him.'

'The mirror took him,' I said.

Eddie translated. The men looked at each other. One of them shrugged.

'*Et alors son miroir a fini par le manger*,' he said.

'*Il le devait une âme*,' said one of the others.

We stood out of the way and they looked through the door, but wouldn't come into the room. Two of them crossed themselves. They went back to the top of the stairs, talked a little in low voices, and left.

'What did he mean about a soul?' I said.

Eddie shook his head. He looked dazed.

'I don't know,' he said. 'Albert owed his mirror one, I suppose.'

He shrugged. I turned back into the room just in time to see Mum going round to the front of the mirror.

'For God's sake don't look in it!' I yelled, but she'd already done so.

'Sorry, darling, but it's just a mirror,' she said. 'Have I done something wrong?'

I suppose it must have been the final straw. I vaguely remember registering that Melly/Melanie had come to and Janice was hugging her down at the end of the room, and that was why Mum had gone wandering off, to leave them alone together, and the next thing I remember was waking up and knowing I was in a hospital even before I opened my eyes, because of the smell. I don't remember this either, but according to Mum the first thing I said was, 'Get the cover on the mirror. Somebody's got to get the cover on the mirror.'

They said it was shock, though I tried to tell them it was just the heat. I expect they were right, but I was ashamed of just passing out like that, when it was all over. Every time I thought about what had happened and how nearly it had all gone wrong I got the shudders, so in the end they gave me a sedative and kept me in hospital all night. Melly too . . . (Don't bother from now on whether I say Melly or Melanie – it's the same person. A lot of people have two names, anyway.)

Mum and Janice had told the doctors that we'd had some kind of terrible shock when we were alone together, and they didn't know what it was, and we'd both passed out. Actually Melly seemed pretty well OK, but she couldn't remember anything that had happened in the room, which was why they kept her in hospital too, but they let us out next morning.

Janice had insisted on staying with Melly and Mum felt the same about me, so they'd slept in chairs by our beds, and Eddie came and picked us all up in the morning, and we went and had breakfast together in the most normal, touristy restaurant we could find. We got a table with a big umbrella out on the pavement in one of the squares, and I told the others what had happened.

Eddie hated it. He really fought against having to believe it. Even with Melly being so obviously Melanie as well, and so happy about it, he still wanted to find some way of thinking that Monsieur Albert had somehow hypnotized us all, me and both girls and both mums and him and the other detective, Pierre, and somehow stolen out with the missing girl, but in the end he gave up.

'All right,' he said. 'Provisionally, and with a lot of misgivings, I'm prepared to act on the assumption that what you say happened actually did. It is still an unholy mess. There is a missing kid I should have reported last night, as far as anyone outside is concerned, and I bloody nearly did so, in spite of Janice and Trish begging me not to. One reason I didn't was that Pierre had found those three types who barged in on us having a drink outside and talking it over, and he managed to settle down at the next table and listen in. They certainly appeared to think that our friend had disappeared into the mirror in the way Keith has described.

'And here is another reason . . .'

He took an old book out of his briefcase and showed it to us. Its cover was some kind of pale leather, the colour of an old dinner-knife handle. He flipped through the pages so that we could see that it was full of a spidery sloping handwriting.

'I found it in the man's bag,' said Eddie. 'I threw the other stuff into the river but I thought I'd better take charge of this in case it told us anything. I was up half the night trying to make head or tail of it. I think it's about three hundred years old. It's mostly in French, with some Latin and a bit of Italian, I think. I thought I might be able to read the French, at least, but it's full of magical jargon and the writing's hell to make out. Almost the only bits I could make sense of are the various headings, which are in capital letters. Look.'

He showed us a page. Even I could read the words at the top. *POUR PREPARER LA CHAMBRE.* To get the room ready.

'What happened to the mirror?' I said. 'Is it safe? Have you got it covered up?'

'In a minute,' he said. 'Let's finish with this. There isn't a title or anything, it just starts straight in. It's a sort of instruction manual for various operations . . .'

He leafed through and read out some of the headings.

'To call out of the mirror one who is trapped in it. To return one to the mirror. To make two from one. To summon from afar the phantasm of one who is trapped in the mirror. To make one enter the mirror and bring out the phantasm . . .'

'Hey! Wait a sec. What's that?' I said, because something, a brown envelope, had fallen out of the book as he turned the page.

'Just a bookmark he was using,' said Eddie. 'Nothing in it except a few bits of hair. Well . . .'

'No, wait,' I said and scrabbled in the back pocket of my jeans. Mum hadn't managed to get back to the hotel for clean clothes for me, so I was wearing the sweaty ones I'd had on yesterday. At least they'd dried out.

I fished out the envelope Monsieur Albert had given me and looked inside. There were some short dark hairs in it.

'Sorry,' I said. 'It's all right. But you remember I told you about him snipping bits off the girls' hair? I just thought . . .'

'Let's have a look,' said Janice, so I passed her the envelope. She shook the hairs out on to her hand and looked at them.

'No, that's not Melly's,' she said. 'It's much too coarse. May I see the other one, Eddie? . . . Yes, that's hers . . . Oh, my goodness . . .'

'That's what he was putting in the cup,' I said. 'I should have remembered he was a conjuror.'

Nobody said anything for a bit. More than anything else that had happened, this gave me the cold shivers. I don't know why.

'I wish I knew what the hell he thought he was up to,' said Eddie. 'And even more how the hell he thought we were going to let him get away with it. But at least it bears out what I was saying. My other reason for not insisting that he has somehow tricked us all is that everything goes to suggest that the man himself believed in the genuineness of what he was trying to do. He was going to do what he'd promised us, though he was also going to cheat us in the end.'

'And he did it,' I said. 'What he'd promised us, I mean. Right, Melly?'

She nodded. It was much easier for us, of course. I'd been there. I'd seen it. I knew it was true. And Melly knew she'd got what she wanted, though she still couldn't remember a thing about how it had happened. It wasn't that hard for Mum either, because she's so good at putting herself in your shoes. When I'd been telling the story she'd practically been in the room with me, living it. But it was much tougher on Janice. It wasn't her kind of thing at all. (I'll put this in here, though it comes later, and I wasn't actually there. Mum told me. It was at the airport. We were going home together because we'd had to change our tickets anyway. I'd gone to look at the bookstore while Mum cruised the duty-free and Janice and Melly stayed with our bags. Mum got back to find Janice alone, because Melly had gone to the toilet. She was crying. 'I keep remembering my other daughter,' she told Mum.

'It's all right when she's here. Then I know I've got them both. But when she's not . . .')

Eddie wasn't so involved, of course, but he still hated it, like I've said, and you can't blame him.

'We're all going to be in very serious trouble if anyone finds out that we've failed to report a missing child,' he said. 'I'm going along with this for the reasons I've told you, but I'm risking my job and my licence to do so. We've all got to get out of here and back to England as soon as we can fix fresh flights, and till then Melly will have to show her face at both hotels, so that questions don't get asked. You'll have to think of a story about why only one girl's flying home – the other one's gone to stay with friends and will be coming home by car with them, or something. And I don't know what the lawyer's going to say about the money he's holding – we'll just have to see. And God knows what I'm going to put in my report.'

'Well, I think you've done wonders,' said Mum. 'I'm sorry we've landed you in this mess, and thank you for being so good about it.'

He shrugged and smiled.

'At least it makes a change from watching people's wives,' he said.

'You were going to say about the mirror,' I said.

'I don't think there's much we can do about that,' said Eddie. 'After I'd got you to hospital I went back to settle with Pierre. I'd left him to see if he could find anything out, and as I've told you he did pick up a bit by listening to the talk outside. But as soon as he went in and tried to ask questions and they realized he'd been with us, they threw him out. He was waiting for me in the square. I went back in on the excuse of wanting to pay for the damage to the door and they threw me out too. It was a woman. She was furious, and frightened, and she wouldn't take any money, and that's all I know. Pierre, by the way, is aware that something pretty rum was up, and he doesn't want to know about it. As far as he's concerned he'd only seen one girl.'

Well, I hung around with Janice and Melly while Eddie and Mum went off to see the lawyer. Luckily he'd already decided for himself that Monsieur Albert was a crook, and, though they couldn't tell him the whole story, anything like, they told him enough for him to agree that, if Monsieur Albert hadn't shown up in a month to claim it, he'd send the money back to Mum. Then we drove around with Eddie and did touristy things and had an amazing meal in the evening to celebrate, and though it was still roasting hot and we ought by rights to have been dead with exhaustion, not to mention nervous as hell that a lot of French cops were going to show up and start grilling us about what we'd done with the missing girl, we didn't bother about any of that. We just talked and laughed and had a really good time.

It was because of Melly. She wasn't wild with high spirits, or anything, but there was this great glow of happiness flooding out of her, so strong that you felt nothing could ever shake or change it. I'd only got to look at her for the stuff that had happened in the Orangerie to sort of fade out and lose its grip. Yes, it had almost gone horribly wrong, but it was never going to, because it had to end like this. This was fixed.

The last thing Eddie said to me when we said goodbye was, 'I'd still like to know how the hell the bastard thought he was ever going to get away with it.'

We all flew back to Birmingham – Mum had a fortnight off and that meant we could go and stay with Melly and Janice at Coventry, and catch up on old friends. When Dad had died Mum had said she never wanted to set foot in Coventry again, but now she really enjoyed herself, and even talked about him sometimes, as if she was getting used to the idea that he wasn't around any more.

The thing I found really hard to take was the idea that Melly and Melanie were one person, not two people who happened to be living in one body. I think I could have coped with that. It was easy for Janice once she got home and settled in to all her usual ways. As far as she was concerned she'd got Melly back, happy and full of life, and Melly helped by just being Melly for her, not smoking or swearing, and she hung around with her old crowd again. She kept her Melanie hairdo, but she'd been nagging for months to be let have it cut like that, and Janice might have given in anyway.

It wasn't hard for Mum, either, though she'd got fond of Melanie at Bearsden. The business about this being both of them didn't seem to bother her. That's how it was, and if Melly was happy with it, she was too.

It was different for me. I'd always been fond of Melly. I'd missed her when she wasn't there, and if she'd come up to visit us in Bearsden I'd have been glad to have her around and sorry when she left. But when Melanie had been living there with us I'd been a lot more than just glad – there'd been something about her which really got me going, something – I don't know – dangerous. (Actually I think there must have been about Melly too, only she didn't let you see it.)

I used to nag away at this when we were alone together. I couldn't help it. I wasn't going to tell her straight out how I felt, but I kept noticing little things that reminded me, and saying something about them. For instance, we were washing up and I passed her a cup to dry and she'd switched hands since the last cup – she was good as ambidextrous now – and I said something about that as if I was joking but she didn't answer. Then, when I was doing the next cup I realized she'd stopped drying so I looked up. She was watching me half sideways, smiling that Melly smile.

'I ken weel what you're effing thinking, you poor wee laddie,' she said.

I felt myself blushing like a beetroot. She laughed and kissed me on the cheek but my hands were all covered with soapy water and I couldn't grab her, and then she was back to being Melly.

She came up to Bearsden for her half-term. (Janice was working and stayed in Coventry.) Scottish half-term wasn't the same as English, so the first two days we only got the evenings together, and the first of them Mum was there so we just sat around and talked. She was different in Bearsden, not just Melly or Melanie, but somewhere between, and older-seeming, very sure of herself without having to prove it to anybody, the way you felt Melanie had needed to.

The second evening Mum said she had to work late. Melly'd got tea ready by the time I was home and she put it on a tray and took it into the lounge so that we could sit on the sofa and pretend to watch telly and have a really good cuddle. That was great. God, I was happy.

After a bit she said, 'You remember that dream I told you?'

'The nightmare, you mean? About the man taking you across a big field towards a travelling cage with some kind of monster in it?'

'Aye. I had it again.'

'Oh . . . That sounds bad. Does it mean . . . ?'

'No. It was just the once, and I won't have it any more. I'll tell you. I was a bairn again, and watching Papa feed his lions, and I went wandering off but there was nobody with me. There was this big field, and over the far side one of the travelling cages, so I went to see. The door was open, so I climbed the step and looked inside, but there was nothing there except this old mirror with its glass all broken. I looked at it a while, and then I said to myself, "I must go and find Papa and show him." That's what I'll be doing tomorrow.'

'Going to Edinburgh?'

'Aye. It's a thing I must do, and I didn't need the dream to tell me. Do you ken how old I am?'

'Trick question. Not fourteen, anyway?'

'Twenty-eight years I've lived in my two bodies, and I'm not shutting any of them away, or it'll be like having a room in my house I'm scared to go into because there's a boggle in it.'

'Can I come too?' I said. Next day was Saturday, and Sunday she was off back to Coventry.

'I was hoping you'd say that,' she said. 'We'll tell Trish we're going to Edinburgh, and she'll get the wrong idea, think it's for a sentimental visit to where we met up.'

'She doesn't know anything.'

'She does, too. Got eyes in her head, hasn't she? Bet you couldn't sit still, last few days before I showed up. Why do you think she stayed away tonight?'

'Anyway it isn't the wrong idea,' I said.

'Maybe not,' she said.

Then, later, I said, 'Are you going to tell him what happened at the Orangerie? You still don't remember any of that?'

'Nothing. I'll just tell him what you told me.'

'I've worked out a bit more, if you're interested.'

134

We hadn't talked about this hardly at all since we'd left Arles. She hadn't wanted to know. But I'd been over and over it with Mum and I'd been down to the main library in Glasgow and read everything I could find about *doppelgänger*s and magic mirrors and so on.

'All right,' she said.

'It isn't about what actually happened,' I said. 'It's about what Monsieur Albert thought he was trying to do. You remember Eddie reading those bits out of the book while we were having breakfast? And then I interrupted him by asking about the envelope with the hair in it?'

'Yes – but I wasna paying a lot of heed.'

'Well, one of them was "To make two from one". That's what he did when you were a baby, and I bet there was something in it about how it only lasts for seven years, or fourteen, or whatever, and then the two have to come together again. And there were two others. One was about summoning the phantom – no, the phantasm – of someone who's trapped in the mirror, and one about making someone go into the mirror and bringing out the phantasm. That's what he was doing when I stopped him. You'd have been in the mirror and your phantasm would have been outside, and he'd have passed the phantasm over to us and we'd have thought it was you. It would have been just like you and talked like you, and it might have been a bit dopey but we were used to that, and it wouldn't remember anything, like you don't, and I wasn't supposed to have seen

135

anything that mattered. And then Mum would have paid him the money and we'd all have gone home, and after a bit he'd have called your phantasm back. I don't think it would just have disappeared. I think it would have died, and we'd have buried it and all been very sad, but if we'd dug down and opened the coffin there wouldn't have been anything in it. I found a story like that in the library.'

She thought about it.

'Aye,' she said. 'And that's why Papa took me away. And that's what Monsieur Albert would have been doing so late of a night in his caravan, calling his toys out of his mirror, and playing with them any way he wanted. Oh, Keith, it was lucky for me you were in the room with me!'

She was leaning against me, very cosy, but I took her by the shoulders and pushed her away and held her.

'Now, listen,' I said. 'OK, it was lucky, and OK you're grateful, but this isn't anything to do with that. I'd have done that for anybody, for Ken, for somebody I didn't know at all. It's over, and you're grateful, and that's OK. But *this* is because I really like you, and I'd feel the same if none of that stuff in Arles had ever happened. But if you're just doing it because you think you owe it to me, then I'm not interested.'

She grinned at me.

'Dinna fret yourself, Keith,' she said. 'I like you fine. This evening.'

*

The coach was just getting in to Edinburgh when she said, 'If this goes right, I'll be coming back here.'

'Leaving Coventry? What will Janice . . . ?'

'No, I get along fine with Mum,' she said. 'In fact I was wrong when I told you she didn't feel like a ma – or maybe she always knew inside her there was something missing between us, and now we've found it. She's great, and I wouldn't change her for Trish, even. But still I'm not letting go of Edinburgh, and Annie's and all. I'll be having as much of that as I can fit in, maybe only a couple of weeks of waitressing in the holidays, but that will do fine.'

'What about your dad? Won't he still . . .'

'Not if today goes right, he won't.'

I didn't try to tell her she was mad. I didn't even think that. If anybody could do it, she could. And maybe she'd arrange to come to Edinburgh by way of Bearsden. And maybe . . .

'Can Annie use an extra waiter?' I said. 'OK, I'm way under age, but so are you.'

We got in in the middle of the morning and went straight to Annie's, so as to be there before it was busy with customers. It wasn't much of a day for tourists, anyway, in spite of it being Saturday – October, and a thick chill drizzle falling.

Monsieur Perrault was the only person in the restaurant when we went in. He had his back to the door and was polishing glasses and putting them on the shelf, but he turned to see who it was and stood

137

there, staring. I stayed by the door while Melanie walked between the tables and waited in the middle of the room.

He finished the glass he was holding and put it carefully with the others, and then came out round the bar. His right hand was clenching and unclenching by his belt. His face was almost white. I could see a blue vein on the side of his head bumping in and out as he walked heavily towards her. She looked him in the eyes and took a pace to meet him. I heard her say something in a low voice.

His eyes widened. He stopped. His hand dropped to his side, but the blue vein went on pulsing.

He said something – a question. She answered, only two or three words.

He turned and put his arm on the bar and bent his head, shaking it slowly from side to side.

I must have been holding my breath all this while, because now I noticed I was letting it go. I should have known it was going to be all right, I thought. She is the lion tamer's daughter.